OUTCASTS

OF

TROUBLESOME CREEK

A Jesse Garnett Western

R. Annan

One Vision Publishing

Outcasts of Troublesome Creek
Copyright 2017 © by R. Annan
WGA Reg. #: R32143 (01/30/17)

Author's Portrait: Hazel Tertsakian
Editor: Karren Doll Tolliver
Photography © L. Annan

One Vision Publishing
Published 2017
ISBN: 978-1-942338-66-6 (eBook)
ISBN: 978-1-942338-65-9 (Print)

Dedicated to the Old Time Radio Club Time Machine

Mickie, Nancy, Butch, Barbara, Tom, Annie and John

Chapter 1

"How's it going, old timer?" asked the newly arrived young man from the city. He'd been in Troublesome Creek for nearly two weeks and like all the other greenhorns, he was eager to stake his claim.

"Tolerable when the pain don't act up," the old prospector replied as he looked the intruder over. His back was hurting. Panning and digging for gold, from sunup to sunset seven days a week, was no work for someone his age. Almost seventy years of age, he'd been prospecting most of his life, except for the time when he was a cowboy, and, later, a chuck wagon cook. Some mornings his back hurt so much he had to drink half a bottle of whiskey for breakfast before going out to work.

"All alone?" the young man asked as he looked around, taking measure of the small claim site. He didn't know the first thing about panning for gold. All he knew was that it was a yellow metal that was worth money and he wanted all he could get. So far that amounted to nothing.

"Yup," the old man replied.

"It must be pretty lonesome, with just you," the young man said, just to keep the conversation from dying.

"Shucks, no, I'm a-doin' jest fine. An' they ain't nobody around ta give me no back talk," the old man said with a chuckle.

The old man studied the newcomer. He'd seen men like him a hundred times before. They came from everywhere, cities, towns and farms, all looking to strike it rich. Most left poorer than when they came. Many of them died face down in the muddy street of Troublesome Creek. These unfortunate ones ended up in the unmarked graveyard on the hill because nobody came to claim their bodies. Just another hole in the ground for the grass to grow over. Troublesome Creek was a cruel, heartless, godless place with no law except the gun.

The old man felt sorry for this one. He seemed like a good person. It was evident he was on his last leg. He figured the man needed money to go back to where he came from.

He'd work cheap just to keep from starving. And he was right. The young man was down to his last penny.

"If yer lookin' fer work, I kin give ya a eagle a day. Take it or leave it."

Before coming to Troublesome Creek, the man, John Stanton, had worked as a skinner in a meat processing plant on the west side of St. Louis. After ten years of handling the bloody, smelly cowhides, he couldn't stand the job anymore. He hated going to work in the morning.

One day, while reading a newspaper article, he saw a way to escape his drudgery. It took a little thought and imagination, but he finally saw a way out of his dilemma. He gathered his wife and two children in the kitchen and told them he had a dream.

"It was like a vision," he said. "I was panning for gold and found a nugget as big as my fist!" He made a fist to show them how big the nugget was.

His wife smiled and said, "It was only a dream, dear."

Stanton pulled the newspaper out of his back pocket and opened it to an article about a place called Troublesome

Creek, south of Sharon Springs, in west Kansas. He spread the newspaper out on the kitchen table for all to see.

"Just look at that!" Stanton said, pointing to a picture taken at an assayer's office in Sharon Springs. It showed a gold nugget as large as a small rock in the hands of a prospector. The article told stories of people going to Troublesome Creek poor and leaving rich overnight.

Stanton tried to convince his wife that the dream was a sign from above, a call to action. A large nugget was waiting for him in Troublesome Creek. All he had to do was go there and get it and they would be rich.

The article explained how simple and easy panning for gold was. No special equipment was needed. In fact, with just a frying pan, many people were finding gold dust by the ounce and more. With a shovel and a wheelbarrow, it was even easier.

At first Jayne Stanton was totally against the idea. She didn't want to risk spending what little money they had on such a risky venture. But John, with the help of the children, finally won out.

Using up most of their savings, he bought an old mule and a small buckboard. He loaded a one person tent on the back of it with some blankets and a wooden crate with canned fish, meat, vegetables, and fruit. In a smaller crate were cooking and eating utensils. He also included an old, rusty shovel and a frying pan.

John Stanton was ready and eager to embark on his great adventure. His wife, Jayne, and his two children, Ken, age 15, and Joy, 17, stood in the door of their cold-water flat on the south side of St. Louis and waved goodbye to their father.

"Write often, dear!" Jayne cried out as he rode off.

"Every day!" he shouted back at her. At that moment, he felt free as a bird. He had suddenly shed the burden of fatherhood and it felt exhilarating.

Luck was with Stanton and he reached Troublesome Creek without any trouble on a clear summer day a month after deserting his family. The place was a madhouse. People were coming in from everywhere to try their luck alongside the raging waters of this branch of the Smokey Hill River that was twelve miles south of Sharon Springs, close to the Colorado border.

For the first time since he was a single man, John Stanton felt unchained. Suddenly all the pressures of work and marriage seemed to wash away in the sparkling, fast-flowing waters of the creek.

No longer did he have to trudge to work in that smelly place he hated so much. No longer did he have to answer to others. Now he could do whatever he wanted, whenever he wanted. Lust and abandon hung in the air of Troublesome Creek like a fever, and John Stanton quickly became infected. This was the life he had longed for before he had married.

Troublesome Creek was one big, ongoing, never ending orgy. It had everything Stanton dreamed it would have, whiskey, women and, best of all, gold. Everyday someone struck it rich, and that was all it took to keep the others digging and panning along the creek bank. It was enough to keep hope alive in Stanton.

But after a week, Stanton couldn't find a free site to pan for gold. If one did become available, he was too slow to react. When he finally found the site, it was taken. He began to worry. By the second week, Stanton's money and provisions were getting critical, both were about to run out. Things finally got so bad he had to sell the buckboard and the mule. Even that money quickly evaporated because everything was so expensive.

That's when he noticed a solitary old man bent over digging for gold by the creek, in the shade of a big cottonwood. Only the old man and no one else.

Stanton's mind took a twisted turn. The gold fever had gotten to him. He saw himself in the old man's place, panning and getting rich. The painted ladies over in the town saloons would take notice, especially at the upscale Purple Dove Saloon. The young man saw himself there at the roulette wheel, flush with money, gambling and drinking, dressed in an expensive suit and wearing a gun like the gamblers did. Everyone in town wore a gun, it seemed.

Stanton was just about at the end of his rope when the old prospector offered him a job. "Sure, I guess I could take it," Stanton said, trying not to sound overly eager, as if he were doing the old man a favor. An eagle a day wasn't much, but it would keep him afloat until his luck changed.

For the next few weeks the old man, whose name was Abner Holmes, taught Stanton the proper way to pan for gold. He had him do all the hard work, digging and shoveling the hard, rocky dirt at the back of the site, near the big cottonwood tree.

Stanton would fill the wheelbarrow, push it up a ramp and dump it in a sluice box. Next he would fill a large pail with water from the creek, carry it up the ramp and dump it in the box to wash the silt away, leaving only the pebbles and rocks. Then he would go back and dig up another load of dirt while the old man examined the box for gold nuggets or dust. It was hard work and Stanton did it ten hours a day, seven days a week, working like a dog.

The old man continually nagged him for being slow. "Put yer back into it, man! We ain't got all day!"

Stanton was kept so busy he never got to see how much gold he was digging out of the earth, but he knew it was considerable. The old man put it in a sack and hid it in his tent. All Stanton got was an eagle. It was almost as if the old prospector were trying to break his spirit, to crush his will.

"No, no, no!" old Abner would bellow at Stanton if he didn't do something exactly the way he was told. "That's not how I told ya ta do it! You ain't got the brains of a river rock, an' thet's fer sure!"

Stanton gradually came to realize all the freedom he first felt when he came to Troublesome Creek was being squeezed out of existence. The old man was leaning hard on him, making him obey his commands. By the end of six months Stanton felt his free will had been taken away and he was nothing but a slave.

He was ready to quit but realized he couldn't. The eagle a day was just enough to pay for his food and drink at the prices charged in the gold field. In effect, he was trapped. There was no way out, except for doing the unthinkable. Unable to bear up under the pressure anymore, the unthinkable became the means to an end.

One night Stanton lay in his tent holding a large rock he had found at the edge of the creek. It was a beautiful rock, smooth and pale gray and shaped like a perfect oval, created and formed in a slow process over an eternity of time. It was a wonder of nature to behold. As he lay in bed feeling the heft of the rock, staring at it, he waited for the sound of snoring to stop coming from the old man's tent. It finally ceased after midnight. Stanton let out an anguished moan, crawled out of his little tent and snuck quietly into the larger one. Once there, he bashed the old man's head in with the beautiful rock.

After getting over the shock of what he had done, Stanton drug Abner Holmes's body down to the creek. He stood watching as the strong current took it twisting and turning southwest toward the Colorado border, ten miles away. He returned to the old man's tent to get the rock. It was covered with blood and not beautiful anymore. Stanton stared at it one last time, shuddered and tossed it into the creek. He stood there in the dark sobbing for a long time then crawled back into his tent.

In a few days, after justifying and reconciling himself with his conscience, Stanton felt better. He should have felt some sort of regret for his act, but he didn't. He now had the old prospector's sack of gold dust and nuggets. After cashing some of it in at the Gold Exchange, Stanton visited the bawdy house and then the saloons. He went on a binge of drinking and frolicking, and the painted ladies of Troublesome Creek came to like and favor him.

Far away, in St. Louis, Stanton's wife and two children waited anxiously for word from him. He had never once written and they were at wit's end worrying about him. "I should go look for Dad," young fifteen-year old Ken Stanton told his mother.

She laughed nervously at the very thought. "No, you can't do that, son."

"Sure, I can, Mom," Ken said. He was a strapping big boy.

"No, you can't, and I'll hear no more talk like that from you. Understand?"

"Yes, Momma," Ken said sheepishly, glancing at his smaller but older sister, seventeen-year old Joy.

That night, after midnight, the two children packed a sack of food and snuck out of the house. They walked across town to their Uncle Fred's place. Uncle Fred delivered furniture for a department store in his buckboard when he was sober, which wasn't often. He kept some tools and a shotgun in the buckboard boot. He used the shotgun to hunt wild rabbit and squirrel outside of town on weekends.

While Uncle Fred lay in bed drunk, Ken and his sister, Joy, hitched up Uncle Fred's horse to the buckboard and rode out to look for their father.

Chapter 2

Much of the gold found in Troublesome Creek was spent buying supplies, basic staples and equipment, all at inflated prices. A meal cost from five to ten dollars, depending on whether it was breakfast or dinner. Getting an aching tooth pulled cost fifteen dollars. A two-bit shot of rotgut whiskey went for a dollar. But a lot of money was also spent in the pursuit of pleasure. Gambling, alcohol and women got a good chunk of it.

An ounce of gold was officially worth about nineteen to twenty dollars. It could be exchanged at one of the many banks in Sharon Springs, twelve miles north, for bank notes or gold coins called eagles. The eagles started at $2.50 for a quarter eagle on up to $10.00 for a full eagle. A gold double eagle was worth $20.00. Eagles and smaller coins such as two-bit quarters, were the most used for many reasons. They looked official, were durable and had a nice ring when you tossed one on the bar and ordered a drink. Eagles were the unofficial coin of the realm in Troublesome Creek. Two-bits didn't buy you much there. Whatever the form of the money, it was the gold behind it that kept Troublesome Creek's wheels greased and rolling.

However, no one liked walking around carrying sacks of gold. They were cumbersome and very heavy. To solve that problem, there was a place in Troublesome Creek where the prospectors could change the yellow stuff into hard cash. It was simply called the Gold Exchange. In the past, there were two such places but one suddenly closed after its owner mysteriously disappeared. That left a man named Mark Fox to run the only exchange in Troublesome Creek. It was located on the main street of town.

Although the official rate of exchange in Sharon Springs was twenty dollars an ounce, in Troublesome Creek, Fox offered only sixteen. Since Fox ran the only exchange in town, most of the prospectors took the sixteen dollars rather than travel the outlaw-ridden, twelve mile road north to Sharon Springs and back. If they needed the money immediately for food or whiskey, or had a certain painted lady waiting, they took Fox's deal and kept quiet. Besides, the bank in Sharon Springs made the prospectors sign all kinds of paperwork.

Fox also played another game. He short-scaled the prospectors by twenty percent, giving him an extra bonus. If someone questioned his honesty, Fox's answer was short and clear, "Take your dust elsewhere, my friend." This usually ended the dispute in Fox's favor. Most of the prospectors were illiterate and couldn't read or write. A lot came in drunk and didn't know their rear ends from their elbows.

Fox kept a good amount of cash in a safe at the Gold Exchange. Whenever he fell low, he would close up shop and go to Scott City with a quantity of raw gold and exchange it at twenty dollars an ounce for bank bills and eagles. He would take the profit and put it in his private account at the Scott City Cattlemen's Saving and Loan Bank where he already had a tidy sum.

Fox stayed clear of Sharon Springs because he didn't want anyone poking their noses into his business in Troublesome Creek. The authorities there might send the law down to check his scales and look at how he operated. That wouldn't be good for business. They could close him down and he'd have to pack up and look for another gold field to set up shop.

As it was, business in Troublesome Creek was booming for Mark Fox. Whenever a troublemaker came complaining about the rate of exchange, Fox would have his guard, Frank Kegan, show him to the door. One day a new prospector brought in a bag of dust. It weighed a hefty five ounces. When Fox gave him eighty dollars, the man complained.

"Shouldn't it be a hundred?" the man asked. "Twenty an ounce is the going price, isn't it?"

"I only give sixteen," Fox said. "If you don't like it, take your dust up to Sharon Springs, mister."

This was his standard reply and it usually worked. However, when this man gave him a hard look, it bothered him. He wasn't one of the usual dummies, and he dressed like a man from the city, even if he looked seedy. After the man left, Fox looked worried. He turned to Frank Kegan and asked, "What do you think, Kegan?"

"I think he's gonna be trouble," Kegan replied. "He might be from Sharon Springs."

"You think they sent him down here to get the goods on me?"

"Maybe. Maybe somebody complained to the authorities up there."

"I hope not. If he is, you'll have to take care of him."

Kegan nodded. He was a tall, slim, broad-shouldered man dressed in black from top to bottom. He wore his wide brimmed Stetson tilted downward, covering his cold, blue eyes. He was a handsome man with a neat mustache above his upper lip that intrigued the ladies. When he took his hat off, his black, wavy hair formed a widow's peak on his forehead.

Fox, the complete opposite, was short and a bit chubby. He wore an expensive, tailor made suit with a starched white shirt and a string tie. This gave him a look of authority and prestige. His face was round and he had brown hair, gray eyes and a puckered mouth that resembled a fish out of water, sucking for air. Anyone seeing Fox for the first time usually took him for a businessman.

The man returned several times, each time complaining about the low rate of exchange that Fox offered him. When he didn't come back for a week and business dropped, Fox got suspicious and had Kegan check into it. It turned out the man was John Stanton from St. Louis and he was making a run to Sharon Spring on behalf of the prospectors. He would write each man's name on his sack of gold dust, cash it in at Sharon Springs, put the money in each man's sack and return with it.

"He's out at Abner Holmes' site" Kegan said. "I checked."

"What happened to old man Holmes?" Fox asked.

"Good question. No one seems to know."

Fox chuckled. "I bet this Stanton knows."

Kegan nodded, but said nothing. He waited, knowing what Fox was going to ask of him. He knew it, but he wanted Fox to say it anyway. This made it Fox's idea, not his.

"He's got to be stopped," Fox said.

Kegan merely nodded and said nothing, waiting for it to come.

"Can you stop him… permanently?"

Again, Kegan kept silent, only nodding his answer. He knew what Fox was saying. He wanted Stanton dead. This was what Fox paid him for, to protect and guard the business. Kegan had killed to protect it before, in other places. Outlaws sometimes came to rob the Gold Exchange. Fox would have been dead long ago if it hadn't been for Kegan's fast gun. Now Fox wanted a man dead who threatened to expose his crooked ways. If Kegan refused, Fox would fire him and send him packing. Fox paid him well and the job was easy and suited him, so Kegan was hesitant to refuse. Someday he'd leave Fox, but not right now.

"Sure," Kegan said. "I can stop him permanently, if that's what you want." He said it as if he didn't like the idea very much.

"Then do it," Fox said sharply, as if Kegan were more of a servant than an employee.

Kegan nodded and walked over to Fox's desk. Without asking, he took a cigar from the humidor and lit it. He walked back over to the window, blew a cloud of smoke and looked out on the main street of Troublesome Creek. He didn't look happy. Fox noticed but said nothing.

Chapter 3

Five miles east of Sharon Springs, former bank robber and ex-convict Jesse Garnett noticed two people standing beside a buckboard up ahead on the road. As he came closer, he saw they were a young boy and a young girl. Garnett brought his big appaloosa to a halt about fifteen feet away, eased out of the saddle and walked over to see what the problem was. The left rear wheel had come off the buckboard. Somehow the cotter pin had worked loose. This allowed the axle nut to vibrate off and the wheel to drop free.

The boy was straining to raise the back end of the buckboard while the girl tried to shove the wheel back onto the axle. Neither one of them were having any luck. When he saw Garnett, the boy stopped struggling and stepped away from the buckboard. The girl held the wheel in front of her as if trying to hide behind it. The boy got a shotgun from the front of the buckboard and pointed it at Garnett.

"Whatta you want, mister?" he said. "We ain't got no money. We was already robbed."

Garnett smiled. "Maybe I can help," he said.

"We don't need no help," the boy growled.

"Yes, we do, Ken," the girl whined. "We can't do it. It's been two hours and we can't get it done. We need help."

"No, we don't," the boy insisted. He sneered at Garnett. "Keep a-goin', mister!"

Garnett put his hands up and backed away. "Sure, kid, whatever you want."

He turned and walked back to his horse. Just as he was about to step into the stirrup, the boy shouted at him. "Hold it, mister!" Garnett heard the boy cock the hammer on the shotgun. He turned around to look. "You come back here," the boy said angrily.

"Sure," Garnett said. He walked slowly over to the buckboard.

"Lift 'er up!" the boy commanded.

Garnett stared at the boy for a moment then nodded. "Alright," he said as he grabbed the back of the buckboard and lifted it up.

The boy handed the shotgun to the girl. "Keep it on him, Joy." The girl took the shotgun and the boy slipped the wheel in place. He quickly put the washer and nut back on. When he was finished, Garnett lowered the buckboard until it sat firmly on the ground. The boy took the gun back from the girl.

The girl stared at the wheel and said, "It ain't got no cotter pin, Ken. It'll come right off agin."

Garnett said, "You got any horseshoe nails?"

"Yeah, we got a couple. Why?" the boy asked.

"Use a horseshoe nail."

"How will that work?"

"Get me a nail and a hammer," Garnett said, "and I'll show you."

The boy nodded to the girl and she went to a small wooden crate in the front of the buckboard, under the bench. She came back with a horseshoe nail and an old hammer. She handed them cautiously to Garnett.

Getting down on his knees, Garnett looked at the axle nut for a moment then turned it to line up the hole in it with the hole in the axle. Once he had them in alignment, he inserted the horseshoe nail. It went half way in then stuck. Garnett took the hammer and pounded it the rest of the way in then bent both ends so it wouldn't fall out again. Standing up, he tossed the hammer into the buckboard.

"That'll hold you until you get to the next town," Garnett said.

"Thanks, mister," the girl said.

Garnett stared at the children. They looked tired and worn. "Where's yer mommy and daddy?" he asked the boy.

"None of yer business," the boy said with a scowl.

"Dad's in Troublesome Creek and we're going ta find him," the girl blurted out.

Garnett nodded. "Well, good luck, then." He started to walk away.

"Hold it!" The boy jumped in front of Garnett and shoved the barrel of the shotgun against his stomach.

Garnett raised his hands. "Hey! Easy with that thing, boy. It might go off!"

"Never mind that! Give me yer money or I'll blast ya."

"What?"

"You heard me! Do it!"

"Sure, kid," Garnett replied. "Take it easy, now." He had been completely caught by surprise. It took a few seconds for him to realize the boy meant business. He smiled. "Whatever you say."

Garnett reached into his front left pocket and pulled out a handful of double eagles. The boy's eyes widened. "Take it, Sis," he said. The girl ran over and snatched the coins from Garnett's hand. "How many?"

The girl quickly counted them. "Eight double eagles."

"That's good. Now get his horse." As the girl ran to Garnett's horse, the boy reached over and pulled Garnett's Colt from its holster. "I'll take this." He stuck it under his belt.

"You need yer butt spanked, kid," Garnett said. "Didn't yer momma teach you better?"

"Shut up about my ma, mister." The boy watched as the girl led the appaloosa over to the buckboard. "Tie it on, Joy."

The girl grabbed the reins of the appaloosa and led it over to the back of the buckboard and tied it up. After that, she climbed up on the bench. "Let's go, Ken."

The boy backed away from Garnett, keeping the shotgun aimed at him.

"You just broke the law, kid," Garnett said.

"Yeah? Well we ain't ate in two days, so I don't give a darn about the law," the boy replied as he walked to the buckboard. "Make one move an' I'll plug ya, mister!"

"Can I at least have my saddlebags? My medicine kit is in it."

"No, ya can't have yer saddlebags," the boy replied.

"What if I said, 'pretty please'?"

"Oh, give him the darn saddlebags, Ken!" the girl said. "An' let's go before somebody comes along."

The boy went to the appaloosa and untied the saddlebags. Instead of handing them over, he threw them into the woods then jumped up on the bench next to the girl. She snapped the reins and the buckboard moved quickly down the road at a fast pace, pulling the appaloosa along with it.

Garnett waited a moment, then went into the woods for his saddlebags. When he walked back out on the road the buckboard was a small object in the distance. He shook his head and cursed at himself for being taken like a greenhorn from the city. With the saddlebags over his shoulder, he held onto them tightly as he walked west towards Sharon Springs. They had six thousand dollars in a secret pocket, all honestly come by.

Chapter 4

In his younger days, when he was a cowboy, Jesse Garnett would bed down at night during a trail drive far away from towns and dream of playing poker in saloons and dancing with painted ladies. Now, after serving four years in prison for robbing banks, he was more apt to dream of busting big rocks into smaller ones.

As he walked along the road to Sharon Springs, Garnett thought about his last bank robbery, about five years ago. He was in his late twenties and had been a cowboy since the age of seventeen. One day, on the drift, he met a certain fellow in a bar in Ellis. This fellow had been a cowboy once, too. They took to liking each other and the fellow talked him into joining the Flint Dyer gang, a small time bank and train robbing outfit.

One of the members of the gang was a man who had been a doctor, but had lost his license over a botched operation. The doctor had a drinking problem and what was supposed to be a simple operation went wrong. His name was Burrows. After drifting here and there and patching up wounded outlaws, Burrows ended up with the Flint Dyers gang. He became Garnett's best friend.

Garnett chuckled as he walked along. It didn't seem funny then, but now it kind of tickled him as he thought of that day his horse tossed him. The gang robbed a bank in Hays City and a posse was on their tail. Garnett's horse hit a rough patch of road and went tumbling down. It quickly got up and left Garnett sitting there for the posse to scoop up. After a quick trial, he was sent to Storeyville Prison. He served four years of a seven year sentence at hard labor. Doc Burrows was the only one to greet him when he walked out a free man.

Garnett's thoughts turned to the boy and his sister. She was a pretty young girl, and that worried Garnett. Some slick operator could make a move on her. The boy had no idea what was waiting for him at Troublesome Creek. It was no place for either him or the girl. It was full of bottom feeders, thieves, murderers and scoundrels who preyed on the weak. He was also worried about his horse. The big appaloosa had been given to him by Doc Burrows the day he got out of prison. He loved that animal and wanted it back.

The closer Garnett got to Sharon Springs, the heavier the traffic got. People on foot, on horseback and in buckboards were coming in from side roads and trails, heading in the same direction as he was. The main road here was clogged and he found himself stuck in a slowly moving human river. A few miles further west, the road was intersected by one that ran south to Troublesome Creek. The road into Sharon Springs itself was packed tight with people looking for lodging and supplies. It seemed as if the whole world were marching towards the Troublesome Creek gold field.

At this point, Garnett was glad he was on foot. Holding onto his saddlebags, he squeezed through the bottlenecks and chokepoints and reached the outer limits of town. Once there, he stopped to look around for a place to eat. All the beaneries he found were full with long waiting lines. He walked up and down several dusty side streets until he found himself in an enclave of strangely dressed people. They spoke a language he was not familiar with and they stared at him as hard as he stared at them. Eventually, he caught the smell of cooking and searched for its source. It was a little eatery inside a courtyard alongside a narrow alleyway. A sign above the door read, "*Sauerbraten*".

There were several well-dressed male and female customers inside when Garnett entered. The men seemed to be business people from Sharon Springs. Some spoke German while others spoke English. None of them wore guns. If they were armed, it was probably with derringers hidden in their clothes. They fastened their eyes on him and whispered. He quickly figured out why. He was covered with dirt and no doubt had a sinister appearance.

Garnett turned slowly and retreated into the courtyard. He sat at a small, empty table outside with the saddlebags hanging over the back of his chair. A woman in a bright, flowery dress and pigtails came out to take his order. She spoke in broken English, explaining the meal of the day. He nodded as she spoke, even though he didn't know what she was saying. When she went away, he had no idea what he had ordered. The smell of cooking from inside the restaurant made Garnett's mouth water.

He waited a long time and was about to leave when she came back carrying a tray with a large plate of steaming food and a long-necked bottle of beer. She put it on the table and left. Garnett stared down at it for a moment then started eating slowly and cautiously. After a few bites he began to eat faster. Soon, he was shoveling food into his mouth like a starved wolf. The food tasted like nothing he had ever eaten before. It was delicious and the beer was cold and strong. For dessert, he had an apple tart and a cup of coffee. After he finished, he rolled a cigarette and sat at the table feeling relaxed and satisfied.

When the lady came with the bill Garnett fished into his saddlebag and pulled out a handful of money. He gave her a ten dollar bill and asked her where he could buy a horse. She went away and came back with his change and a man wearing short, leather pants with suspenders.

"You want a horse?" he asked. His English was better than the woman's.

"Yes," Garnett said, "a horse."

"You want saddle, too?"

"Yes, everything," Garnett said.

The man waved to Garnett as he walked away, saying, "Come with me."

Garnett grabbed his saddlebags and followed the man into the restaurant and through the kitchen. They went down an alley that came out on a street lined with shops. At the end was a pawn shop connected to a barn with a corral attached.

"You go in there and see my son, Karl," the man said. He turned and went back the way they came.

Garnett entered the shop and was immediately amazed. There was an assortment of used equipment such as saddles and saddlebags. Gunbelts, harnesses, and all kinds of tack hung from the walls. A long, glass case held ammunition and guns of all makes and models. Garnett could see horses through the open barn door. The only things the place lacked were hats and boots. A cowboy would never pawn his hat or boots.

Garnett went straight to the glass display case and selected a single action Army Colt and a box of forty-fives. He took the gun, did some fancy twirling and dropped it into his holster. Karl watched with wide, approving eyes.

The saddles took some examining but Garnett found an embossed, single cinch made by a company he knew of in Utah with a good reputation. Finally came a bridle. Garnett chose a hackamore with rosettes.

"How about a horse?" Garnett asked.

"Ya," Karl said. He led Garnett through the door into the barn past bales of hay, into the corral where the horses were.

"You pick," Karl said.

Garnett nodded and stood by the corral fence. There were about a dozen animals, but most of them were cowboy quarter horses, duns, chestnuts, and blacks. He stood there letting them get their nostrils full of his scent, then he whistled. Two quarter horses came over to check him out.

Garnett chuckled. They were good cowboy horses. He picked one and rubbed its neck. It nuzzled him. He checked its brand. It had an over-brand that looked like a Box C that had been made into a Box O.

Garnett chuckled again. "I hope you're not cold backed, my friend." He turned to Karl. "How much for the horse and everything?"

"For all, seven hundred fifty."

Garnett didn't even squabble about the price. He fumbled in one of the saddlebags and pulled out a handful of bills and paid. He got the saddle and tack and left it on a bale of hay near the corral fence.

"In the morning," Garnett said. "I'll come back in the morning."

Karl nodded. "Ya. *Morgen* is okay."

After leaving Karl's place, Garnett found a bed and breakfast down the street by a butcher shop. He rented a room for the night. In the morning, he had breakfast at the restaurant and then went back to Karl's place to get his horse and tack. Noontime found him on the road heading south for Troublesome Creek.

It was a long, slow ride past broken down wagons and buckboards and groups of people on foot carrying heavy backpacks. On some stretches, it was better traveling alongside the road than on it. By three in the afternoon he saw a sign pointing to the right. Troublesome Creek was a mile down, nestled in a flat, open area of hardpan.

What was called a town was basically a makeshift array of hastily built structures located fifty feet from Troublesome Creek. Almost as wide as a river, Troublesome Creek's water raged and roared like an angry lion as it smashed and pounded stubbornly against rocks and boulders, sending a continuous spray of wet mist into the air.

Saloons, bawdy houses and gambling dens lined the main street of Troublesome Creek. Squeezed in between these were various specialty stores and a mercantile. A combined blacksmith shop and stable was located at the entrance of town. There was also a place to change gold dust and nuggets into money. It was called the Gold Exchange. There was also a doctor's office, but no jailhouse.

As for the law, it didn't work in a place as wild as this. The last person who tried to bring justice to Troublesome Creek was murdered months ago. Since then, no one else was brave or crazy enough to give it a second try. The nearest law was twelve miles north, at Sharon Springs. Justice was but an afterthought in Troublesome Creek.

When the gold ran out, and someday it would, Troublesome Creek would become a ghost town overnight. It would become an empty shell and gather dust and rot as the years passed it by. If it was lucky, it would become a footnote in some historian's archive. Gold was its lifeblood, the only thing that kept it alive. Its only hope for survival was if some dedicated, stubborn souls clung to their dream of making it into a town. They might hang on hoping for a miracle, or pray for a stage line to come through.

The first thing Garnett did when he rode into town was to look for his horse. By pure accident he found the buckboard up a side street near the Gold Exchange concession. His horse was still tied to it and the kids were asleep in the back under a blanket. They never heard him sneak up on them as he quietly dismounted and walked over to the appaloosa. The horse was glad to see him and whinnied and snorted.

"Hold it, mister!"

Garnett turned around. The boy was sitting up with the shotgun pointed at him. He crawled stiffly from the buckboard. "Relax, kid," Garnett said. "I brought you a new horse and a gun."

The girl came out from under the blanket and stood beside her brother. She seemed glad to see Garnett. "Hi, mister."

Garnett smiled and tipped his hat. "Howdy, ma'am."

"Can you help us find our daddy?" the girl asked. "We can't find him."

Garnett didn't know what to say. He could see they both looked tired and frightened. "I suppose I could, miss," Garnett said. Then, "Are you two hungry? I'll take you to breakfast, if you are."

"No," the boy said stubbornly.

"Yes," the girl replied. "We're broke an' ain't eaten since yesterday."

"Let's go eat, then," Garnett said.

"Oh, alright," the boy said grudgingly.

Garnett tied the quarter horse alongside the appaloosa on the back of the buckboard and climbed up on the bench with the children. He steered it along the alley and out onto the street. They found a beanery at the end of town near the gold digs. It also had rooms for rent. The sign read "Mary Mason's Beanery, Bed and Breakfast". They could hear the rush of Troublesome Creek's waters somewhere out back.

They tied up at the rail and went in. A middle aged woman with white hair was tending to customers. She finally worked her way to their table. "Howdy. I'm Mary Mason. We got most anything ya want. What'll it be, folks?"

Garnett treated himself, Ken and Joy to ham, eggs, grits and coffee. After they had eaten, Garnett asked Mary for directions to the panning sites.

"Just follow the trail along the creek. The sites stretch for miles and miles on this side. Usually there's a claim sign up with a name on it."

"We're looking for a man named Stanton. John Stanton."

"John? Sure, he used to come in here every day, until a month ago. I ain't seen him since. You might ask some of the prospectors."

Joy started to cry. Garnett said, "You don't happen to know where his site is, do you?"

"No, can't say that I do. Best thing to do is go down to the field and ask somebody."

"Thanks, I'll do that."

They left and followed the trail alongside the creek. All the panning sites were on the east side because of the steep incline and rocky outcrops on the west side. Every four or five sites Garnett would stop and ask about John Stanton. The answer was always the same. "Not here, friend, maybe further down the line."

They went on following the winding creek through pine stands, cottonwood, and willow, stopping again and again. They were a good mile down the trail and were about to give up when they got lucky.

"John? Sure, I knew John," the man said. His wife and son stood looking on.

"Knew?" Garnett asked.

"Yeah," the man said. "He's gone."

"Gone?"

"Yup. One day he jest disappeared."

"Any idea where he went?"

"Nope. The rumor was he was messin' around with one of them bar girls in town an' the boyfriend took revenge. Of course, thet's jest a rumor. Nobody kin prove who did what ta who, bein' as there ain't no law in Troublesome Creek. Heck, he might-a got drunk an' fell inta tha creek fer all anybody knows. Anyway, people disappear around here every day, it seems. Ya git used to it after a while."

"Oh, Daddy!" Joy cried. She started sobbing. Ken put an arm around her.

"Where's his claim?" Garnett asked.

"Three sites down. We're a-watchin' it out of respect, in case his kin should happen ta come."

"They're here," Garnett said.

The man stared at the children and nodded. "I see," he replied sadly. "If we kin help, why, jest let me know."

"Thanks," Garnett said.

They got back in the buckboard and rode further down to where they found a claim sign. Stanton had crossed out Abner Holmes' name and put his below it. His small tent and Holmes' larger tent were still standing. Prospecting equipment was scattered all about. Garnett pulled the buckboard in off the trail and parked it under the big cottonwood tree. There was enough grass there for the three horses to chew on. Joy jumped down, crawled into the larger tent and cried.

Garnett turned to Ken. "Kid, I'll take my gun back. You take this one. The quarter horse is yours, too." They exchanged guns. "Can you shoot, kid?"

"Sure."

"Good. I've got a box of forty-fives you can have."

"Thanks, mister."

"Jesse, kid. Call me Jesse."

"Alright, Jesse, I'm Ken."

Garnett shook the boy's hand. "Look, Ken, I'll give you enough money to go back home, wherever that is."

"I ain't goin' home," Ken said stubbornly. "Not until I find my dad."

"Won't your mother be worrying about you and your sister?"

The boy's face screwed up and he began to cry. "Oh God! Oh, God!" he sobbed and crawled into the tent with his sister.

Garnett stood by the creek listening to their crying. After a few moments, he walked over and knelt by the opening. "Look, kids," he said, "I could stay around for a while. I don't have to go anyplace right now."

The girl replied, "Alright, thank you, mister."

Garnett walked over and stood at the edge of the creek and looked at the roiling waters. He shook his head and muttered softly, "Garnett, what the hell have you gotten yourself into this time!"

Chapter 5

There was a time when Troublesome Creek had two gold exchanges. One was owned by old Seth Hurley and the other by Mark Fox. Hurley offered a higher price per ounce than Fox did. That is, until one day he up and left town.

It was all too sudden to believe. One day Hurley was doing a brisk business and the next day he was gone. No one knew where or why. No one, that is, except Mark Fox and Frank Kegan. Kegan was Fox's hired gunny. He could be very persuasive and one day Fox told him to be persuasive with old Hurley.

"Convince the old fart it's time to retire from the business, Frank," Fox said.

"Permanently or what?" Kegan replied.

"I don't care, as long as he's gone."

One night Kegan went over to Hurley's place and got him out of bed. He slapped him around a bit and even threatened to hurt his wife. That was enough to make Hurly head out to another gold field across the border in Colorado. Kegan even helped him pack.

People disappeared in Troublesome Creek every day and no one fretted about it unless they suspected foul play. With over two thousand strangers crowded like ants into such a small area, it was an everyday occurrence. A lot of these so-called prospectors were robbers and murderers and other dregs of humanity. Good people and bad people worked alongside each other with one purpose, to find gold and become rich.

Whenever Fox ran low on money, he would remove the gold from the big safe behind the counter in the Gold Exchange and put it in a carpetbag. No one would suspect there was gold dust and nuggets under the shirt he placed on top of it. He'd leave Kegan behind to guard the Gold Exchange, in case somebody tried to steal the furniture and safe, and ride his little one-horse buckboard to Scott City.

After cashing in the gold at the assayer's office in Scott City, Fox would take the money across town to the Cattlemen's Bank and deposit a large amount of the money in his account, keeping just enough to run his business on.

No one asked any question because everyone knew Fox came from the gold fields of Troublesome Creek. They were glad to have him as a customer because he deposited large amounts of cash once each month. When business was over, Fox returned to Troublesome Creek a richer and happier man.

For the most part, life at the Gold Exchange went along without any major incidents. Often it was boring for Frank Kegan. Around noontime, the gunman would stand by the window of the Gold Exchange and stare across the street at Grant's Mercantile and Post Office. He did this to pass away the time and to satisfy his curiosity about who came to town and who left. Of special interest was the light passenger coach from Sharon Springs. It brought in both newcomers and the mail. It was fascinating to see who arrived by stage. Mostly it was gamblers, card sharps, carpetbaggers and painted ladies. Once in a great while it was a Bible salesman or a sky pilot. Many times, a new feminine face would appear only to be seen later at one of the local saloons.

One day a woman got off the coach and went into Grant's Mercantile. A few minutes later she came back out and stared in the direction of Fox's Gold Exchange. Then, moments later, she began to walk across the street.

Kegan watched her closely. He liked the build of her, the way she carried herself. She wore plain city clothes, a wide brimmed hat, a light cloth coat over her dress, and city shoes. He was pleasantly surprised when she came up on the porch and walked directly into the Gold Exchange. As she passed close to him he momentarily caught the scent of her. Her face was plain, but she was nice to look at and Kegan's eyes stayed on her as she approached Fox.

"Can I help you, ma'am?" Fox asked, looking up from his desk where he was writing in a ledger.

"Perhaps. Mr. Grant at the store said I should ask you."

"Ask me what?"

"About my husband and children."

Fox looked down at the ledger again and continued writing.

"Ah, what's your husband's name, lady?"

"Stanton. John Stanton."

She never noticed the flicker of panic in Fox's eyes, or the look that flashed across his face. None of his victim's relatives had ever showed up before. It was unexpected and he wasn't prepared to deal with it. He stalled for a moment to get his thoughts in order and control his voice.

"What was his name, again, ma'am?" Fox asked, pretending to be interested.

"Stanton. John Stanton."

Fully recovered, Fox smiled and walked up to the counter. "I'm Mark Fox, Mrs. Stanton." Fox reached across the counter and shook her hand. He looked over at Frank Kegan. "Get Mrs. Stanton a chair, Frank."

"I won't be staying," she said. "I just came to ask about my husband. He came here to look for gold. Mr. Grant said that perhaps you had seen him."

"Well, uh, didn't Mr. Grant tell you, ma'am?"

"Tell me what, Mr. Fox?"

"He should have told you. I'm sure he knew."

Jayne Stanton's face turned pale. "Knew what?"

Fox looked down at his hands to avoid her eyes. "That your husband disappeared a month ago. Mr. Grant should have told you."

Kegan got a chair and carried it over to Jayne Stanton. She slowly sat down, looking like she'd been punched in the gut, but she didn't cry. Their eyes met for a moment and Kegan went back to his post by the window.

"I don't know what you mean. You mean he left here to go someplace else?"

"Well, no. His equipment is all here, everything. So, no, it appears he was...he might have been..." Fox left it hanging.

"You're saying he might have been...killed?"

Fox nodded. "Frank, get Mrs. Stanton a drink, will you?"

Kegan went to the small sideboard near one wall where there were several kinds of alcoholic drinks and poured a shot of brandy in a small glass. He took it to Jayne Stanton. She took a sip, coughed and handed it back to Kegan.

"Thank you, sir." Their eyes met and locked once more.

"Frank," Kegan said. "Frank Kegan, Mrs. Stanton."

"Thank you, Mr. Kegan."

"Should I send Mr. Kegan to hold the stage for you, Mrs. Stanton? You'll probably want to go back to where you came from, I'm sure."

Jayne shook her head. She seemed dazed and uncertain. "No, Mr. Fox. I can't leave yet. My children are here. I have to find them."

Fox stole a glance at Kegan. He didn't expect this turn of events. It was bothersome. "What makes you think they're here, Mrs. Stanton?" Fox asked.

"They ran away over a week ago. They left a note."

Another complication. Fox decided the best thing to do was play the role of the good Samaritan. He had played it many times before and he knew it well.

"Then you must stay and find them, Mrs. Stanton. I'll have Frank help you. Will you help Mrs. Stanton find her children, Frank?"

"Sure, I'd be glad to," Kegan said staring at Jayne Stanton.

"I would be most grateful," Jayne said as she stood up. "Is there a place I can stay in town, Mr. Fox? I'm very tired."

"Frank, take Mrs. Stanton to Mary Mason's Bed and Breakfast. Tell her to charge my account, meals and all," Fox said.

Jayne smiled at Fox. "That's very kind of you, Mr. Fox, but you shouldn't. It's too much."

"Nonsense! I insist, Mrs. Stanton, I absolutely insist!" Fox said, getting into the role of a concerned humanitarian.

"You're very kind, sir."

While this exchange was going on, Kegan stared at Jayne Stanton. He saw a woman who had lived a hard life dedicated to a man who really didn't care about her. While at Troublesome Creek, John Stanton had acquired a reputation as a loose man with cards and women. A rumor connected him to the disappearance of Abner Holmes. Some of the other prospectors thought Stanton had murdered the old man. Stanton told everyone that Holmes had sold his claim to him and left. No one believed it, but Stanton stuck to his story anyway. There was no law in Troublesome Creek to investigate the matter.

Kegan noticed the Stanton woman hadn't cried over her loss. Later, when she was alone, perhaps she would cry. Not over him, but over the wasted years that had finally led her here and now to this horrible place. A place where the damned met their fate by the gun, by knife or in the fast, cold waters of Troublesome Creek.

Jayne Stanton stood up, turned and walked out of the Gold Exchange and up the street with Frank Kegan at her side. As they walked along, she could feel his eyes staring at her. It was strange how, the first time their eyes had met, she had felt a warm glow and an instant liking for this big man dressed in black. She wondered what kind of man he really was. She also felt guilty for not feeling crushed by the news about her husband. Had he run off and left her and the children or had he been murdered? Their marriage never bonded the way a marriage should. Several times they came close to separating. If it weren't for the children, she would have left him long ago.

As they walked along, she glanced at Kegan and wondered if he was a man who would stick by the woman he loved and would be willing to die for her. From what little she had seen of him, he came across as that kind of man. He had stared at her in a certain way, as if he had suddenly found something he had been looking for. A force came from him, making her feel she could place her fate in his hands. She didn't know why, but she felt that way and knew she shouldn't. After all, she had just met him. She was baffled, even embarrassed by her feelings and quickly shut them out of her thoughts. She mustn't think that way about him.

Jayne suddenly realized he was holding her arm in a protective way and it felt good. She looked up at him and smiled.

"Are you alright, ma'am?" he asked.

"I think so," she replied.

They kept walking. People stared at them, smiled and nodded.

Chapter 6

What Mark Fox didn't know was that a certain clerk named Tom Sanders at the Cattlemen's Bank in Scott City took a keen interest in his transactions there. He often handled the entries on Fox's account, recording the sums of money he was depositing and making out the receipts for him. Over a period of time, the clerk came to know who Fox was, where he stayed, and what he did for a living.

A bank clerk's job can be boring or exciting. Sometimes it can also be short lived, like when the bank is being robbed. A smart clerk was the one who handed over the money without hesitation and stayed alive. He wasn't expected to be brave. That was the bank guards' job.

For the most part, Sanders' existence was mundane. Day after day he handled other people's money and wished it was his. At twenty dollars a month, few bank clerks ever got rich sitting behind a teller's cage or desk handling green paper, the stuff that dreams were made of.

When Fox came in once a month and deposited his large sums of money, Sanders wondered what it would be like to be him. The suit that Fox wore would set him back a year's wages. After hours, when the bank closed its doors, Sanders would walk back to his little room in a low class boardinghouse several blocks away. Fridays, however, were different. He would stop at a saloon on the way to his room and spend some time talking to the barman. After a few glasses of beer, the clerk got talkative.

"How was your day at the bank, Tom? Get knocked over agin?" That was the going joke between Sanders and the barman, Phil.

When his bank was robbed a year ago, Sanders was prepared and knew exactly what he had to do to stay alive. He'd gone over it many times in his mind while he lay in bed at night. Dropping on the floor, he pretended to faint. He lay there like a corpse until it was all over and someone came and fretted over him. He faked a slow recovery and was sent home for the rest of the day with pay.

"We weren't robbed today, Phil," Tom Sanders would chuckle. "Maybe next week."

One Friday, Tom didn't notice the two men dressed like cowboys at the bar not far from him. When Phil mentioned the word bank, they perked up and listened carefully to the conversation.

"Yeah, Phil," Tom was saying. "Once a month this guy comes in with a load of cash and puts it in his account. He's been doing it for years. Christ, the guy is loaded!"

"Who is he?"

"His name is Fox. He's runs the gold exchange business at that gold field near Sharon Springs," Tom replied.

"You mean Troublesome Creek?" Phil asked. Tom nodded. Phil continued, "Yeah, I heard about that place. People are getting rich over there."

The two men, Curt Traven and Link Fontaine, who made a living by robbing banks and trains, took all this in. They stood very quietly at the bar sipping their red eye and staring ahead. When they figured they had heard enough, they paid and left.

Two blocks away, at a flophouse, they sat in a dingy little room lit by an oil lamp and talked with Dirk Larsen, their boss, and another cohort, Cory Dupree. They were old time bank and train robbers out of touch with the times. Larsen, a big, grizzly bear of a man and the ugliest, poured drinks all around.

"The clerk said this guy Fox runs a gold exchange in Troublesome Creek," the short one with a beard, Curt Traven, said.

"An' ya say this Fox is loaded?" Larsen asked.

"He must be, boss," Fontaine replied. "He's been loadin' up his account in the Cattlemen's Bank here in Scott City." Link Fontaine was over six feet tall and skinny as a pole bean. His cheekbones were sharp enough to cut paper.

"Maybe we should ride over to Troublesome Creek an' pay this guy a visit," Cory Dupree said. Dupree was a round faced, double chinned man who carried about twenty pounds of extra weight around his belly. He looked like he never wandered too far from the table.

"Why don't we jest grab him the next time he comes down this way?" Traven said.

"That'll be another month. The clerk said he only comes down once a month."

"Yeah," Fontaine cut in. "It ain't but a three day ride west to Troublesome Creek. We could jest mosey up there an' rob him."

"I wonder where he keeps thet gold an' money?" Dupree asked.

Larsen sneered, "He keeps it in a safe, in the exchange, ya darn fool!"

"Shucks," Fontaine said. "Why don't we jest rob the damn bank right here and head fer Texas."

"Mexico is better," Traven said. "Them Mexican women are sweet an' easy."

Larsen scowled. "I've seen thet bank, Fontaine. It's got guards all over, front and back. An' the marshal watches it like a hawk."

"Yeah," Dupree said, "I ain't goin' near thet place."

Larsen refilled the shot glasses. "Yeah, it ain't easy like it was in the old days," he said. "Time was ya could walk into a bank an' they would throw the money at ya. Now they hand it ta ya an' ambush ya on the way out."

Everyone nodded. For a while they sat there thinking about the good old days when robbing banks and trains was almost considered an honest profession. Nobody got hurt then, just the banks and trains. It wasn't like that anymore. Now the big banks and railroads sent detectives after you. They hunted you down, even if you went to Mexico. The rewards were bigger now, and people turned you in.

"Yeah." Larsen finally broke the spell. "Better to rob this Fox guy than the bank. Hell, he might have thousands in thet safe up there at the creek."

They all nodded and took a drink of red eye.

Chapter 7

The old Chinaman Huang Ling, his mother, and his young concubine Mae Wan ran the laundry concession in Troublesome Creek. They came from Peking to San Francisco to set up a business there. It soon became evident to Huang Ling that there were one too many Chinese laundries in that ocean port on the West Coast. Besides that, there were also one too many young Chinese boys who had their eye on his eighteen-year old bride.

When he heard about the place called Troublesome Creek in the region of west Kansas near the Colorado border, he decided to make the long trip there. He wanted to get his beautiful young wife as far away from San Francisco as he could. Anyway, the gold fields seemed like a good place to make money because he could charge higher prices there.

At first he was very happy with this new location even though it was a wild and savage place where men wore guns and shot each other in the streets over insults, women, and cheating at cards.

Of course there were other things he didn't approve of, too. For one, the town was filthy. In the morning the main street was littered with playing cards, whiskey bottles, paper, and horse droppings. Often there were dead bodies as well, but usually these were carted away before they began to rot and smell.

This would not have been allowed back in his home country. And where was the law? There was no law, although a rumor went around saying that a marshal was being sent down from Sharon Springs to tame the place. The rumor kept going, but the marshal never came.

Fortunately, his shop was located in a good place. It was situated right in the center of town across from a gold exchange. There was a barber on his right and a saloon on his left. Huang Ling was lucky to get the spot at all. The previous owner had been a newspaper publisher who, for some reason, found the town not to his liking and left. Perhaps that was because few people in Troublesome Creek could read or write. Drinking and fighting was what they did best.

But the problem here was the same as back in San Francisco. His beautiful young wife attracted undue attention from the male population. He lectured her about wearing provocative clothing and had her cover up her voluptuous body. Finally, he forced her to dress up like a boy, have her hair cut short and wear a hat that covered most of her face. But even then, her lips gave her away. And her slight form and her walk could not be hidden under clothing. The white ghosts, as he called the Americans, were a vulgar people, especially here in Troublesome Creek where they were rude and had absolutely no manners.

However, the prospectors were generous with their money and usually paid his price even though it was high. Especially the man who ran the Gold Exchange across the street. He came with white cotton shirts and fine suits. He even brought his underwear to be washed, unlike the others who never did. Maybe they just never changed that part of their clothing. The savages.

About six months after settling in and establishing his business, Huang Ling began to suspect something was going on with is young bride behind his back. He wasn't sure what it was, but he felt it and saw it in her behavior towards him. Of late, she refused his advances by complaining of headaches or backaches. True, the work at the laundry was hard and the girl labored long hours, from sunup to sunset, seven days a week. But she was young and should be able to stand up to the pressure, just as he, a sixty-five-year old man, did.

Was it another man? There were no other Chinese men in town, so it had to be a white ghost. That would be a disgrace. He could never face his mother with that. Even his ancestors would complain from the grave. His honor would be stained forever.

One night when he awoke to find her bed empty, he came to realize his suspicions were justified. He stayed awake until she returned. She wore only a sheer chemise. "So," he said firmly, "you betray your husband who has been faithful and kind to you. Is that how you thank me for taking you from that lowly village where you were born and were destined to die?"

Mae Wan sneered at the withered up old man. "I wish I was still there with the boy who loved me. But no, you came with your money and bought me like one buys a pig or a chicken, and took me away from those I love."

"If they had loved you, my child, they would not have sold you. They loved money more than you."

"Yes, a girl born to a farmer is useless. Better to sell her even to an old man. I hate all of you."

"Who is this white ghost you meet in the night. Are you afraid to reveal him?"

"What does it matter who he is? All you need to know is that I do not love you, old man, and I never will."

"Oh, I will find out, you know. And when I do, he will be very sorry."

Mae Wan laughed. "Old fool! The one who loves me is big and important in this town. He is far above you. So, be careful, it is better you do not know who he is. Now leave me, old one, I am tired of your ugly face."

For a moment, Huang Ling started to shake with anger. He wanted to reach out and strangle the girl, but fought the urge. He finally calmed down and smiled. "As you wish, my dear, as you wish."

He went back to his room and lay in bed thinking. He thought he knew who the man was. The most important man in town was the man who ran the Gold Exchange, Mark Fox. It had to be him. Yes, he was the big and important white ghost who Mae Wan was consorting with. It could not and must not be allowed to go on.

Chapter 8

"**Y**ou're spending a lot of time with that Stanton woman, Kegan," Mark Fox said. "What's going on?"

At first Kegan didn't answer. He didn't like Fox butting in on his personal affairs. "Nothing. I'm just keeping an eye on her. This is a rough town."

"Well, don't forget, you're working for me, not her." Fox lit a cigar. "Where is she now?"

"Walking around town, asking about her kids."

Fox walked over to the door of the Gold Exchange and looked out through the window. "What a mess. Parents come here looking for their kids, and kids come here looking for their parents. It goes on and on."

"Yeah," Kegan said, "and some of the kids come here to pick pockets, too."

Fox chuckled. Kegan noticed Jayne Stanton coming out of the Chinese laundry. She stood there looking around as if lost. Finally, she walked into a shop next door.

"Christ, she's asking everybody, even the Chinese," Kegan said. He laughed. "I bet they didn't understand a word she said."

Fox chuckled. "The girl does. She picked up the lingo fast."

Kegan stared at Fox. "You'd best be careful there, boss. If the old man finds out about you two, he might come looking for trouble."

"Looking for me? Are you kidding? The old fart is scared of me." Fox paused to shake the ashes off his cigar. "Anyway, she's young enough to be his granddaughter."

"How'd he get her?"

"She says he bought her. Her father was a poor farmer."

"Jesus! They sell their kids?"

"Farmers do, if it's a girl."

Suddenly Kegan lost interest and walked to the door. "Some guy is bothering her," Kegan said.

"It's not your problem, Frank."

"I guess I'm old fashioned that way," Kegan said. He opened the door and went out on the porch.

A rough looking man had Jayne Stanton boxed in down the road, a few yards away. He held her by her left arm. "Come on, baby! Be nice, now. I jest wanna buy you a drink, is all!"

Kegan walked quickly up to them, stopped and tapped the big brute on the shoulder. "Move on, fellah," Kegan said, "the lady isn't interested."

The hairy hulk turned to see who was sticking their nose into his affair. When he saw Kegan, he took an aggressive step towards him. "Who the hell told you ta butt in, mister?"

Kegan reached into his pants pocket and pulled out a double eagle. "Here, take it. The drinks are on me," Kegan said calmly.

The grizzly bear sneered and slapped the coin out of Kegan's hand. He growled, "I'm gonna kick yer ass, mister!"

The giant came at Kegan. He stepped to the right, drew his Colt and swung the butt against the man's left temple. It hit hard with a thud. The man's legs buckled and he sat in the road looking glassy eyed and dazed. He tried to get up but couldn't. Kegan walked around him and up to Jayne.

"Oh, dear! Is he going to be alright?" she asked, looking down at the man.

"He'll be fine," Kegan replied. He took her small hand in his big one and escorted her over to the plank sidewalk. "How about a cup of coffee, Mrs. Stanton?"

"Why, yes, that would be nice, thank you."

As they walked off she glanced back at the man. He was now on his feet and staggering over towards the Purple Dove Saloon.

Jayne and Kegan soon were sitting at a small table in Mary Mason's Beanery, Bed and Breakfast. The road from the gold field ran past it into town. From the window they could see the ebb and flow as people came in and left to go back to their digging sites.

"Thank you for coming to my rescue, Mr. Kegan."

"It was my pleasure, ma am."

Kegan's eye caught hers and held them until she looked away. She smiled as she looked out of the window. "This certainly is a rough town, isn't it?"

"Yes. You should go home, Mrs. Stanton," Kegan said in a concerned voice. He surprised even himself.

She was caught off guard by the suddenness of his words. "I can't, yet," she responded firmly.

"Your children might not be here."

"They left a note."

"Yes. You said that in the Gold Exchange."

"It's true. I have it in my purse. Do you want to see it, Mr. Kegan?"

"No. I didn't mean to upset you. It's just that this is a dangerous place for a woman alone."

"Why should you care, Mr. Kegan? You don't even know me."

He wanted to tell her that he wanted to get to know her better, but held back. That kind of talk wouldn't go over with a woman like her. Especially at a time like this. The loss of her husband still lay heavy on her mind.

She wanted to change the subject, so she said, "How about you, Mr. Kegan? What are you doing here, sir?"

"I work for Mr. Fox."

"Yes. You guard the Gold Exchange. That must be a dangerous job."

"It can be dangerous. We've had a few robberies."

"I can only imagine, what with everybody wearing a gun around here. I suppose you're good with a gun."

"If I have to be, yes."

They heard the sound of a buckboard on the road outside. There were children in it, talking. Jayne Stanton glanced out of the window. What she saw gave her a jolt. She quickly got up and shouted, "Oh, God, there they are!"

"Who?"

"Ken and Joy! My children!"

Jayne ran outside onto the porch waving and yelling at the passing buckboard. It stopped twenty feet down the road. The children looked in her direction then jumped down. They called to her as they scrambled up the porch steps into her waiting arms.

Jesse Garnett sat in the buckboard watching as the mother and children hugged, cried and talked. When they had gotten it out of their system, Joy called her mother's attention to him.

"Mr. Garnett, please join us," Jane said loudly.

Kegan came out to join her and the children. He watched as Garnett turned the buckboard around, brought it back to the beanery, and tied it to the hitching rail.

"I'm Jayne Stanton, Mr. Garnett, and this is a friend, Mr. Kegan."

Garnett saw that Kegan was sizing him up. He returned the favor. They finally shook hands. Each knew who and what the other one was. There was immediate mutual respect.

They went back into Mary Mason's place and sat down. Kegan ordered pie and soda pop for Ken and Joy. There was a lot to be said between the children and their mother, so they talked. They left out the part where they held Garnett up and robbed him, and he let that slide by without a word.

"Your husband's claim is not far from here," Garnett said. "We've been working it every day."

"Mr. Garnett showed us how to pan for gold," Ken said.

"Oh, really, now?" Jayne said. Her voice showed how happy she felt knowing her children were safe and in good hands.

"Yep!" Ken said.

"And, did you find any gold?"

"Yep. Yesterday we found some. When we get an ounce, we're gonna cash it in at the exchange place."

Kegan didn't say much. It came to his mind he was sitting next to the family of the man he had murdered and tossed into the creek for Mark Fox. At that moment he hated Fox, but despised himself more. And, to complicate things, he had deep feelings for her, a woman far above the painted ladies he usually consorted with. The way she held herself, her way of talking, set her high above any woman he had ever known.

How could Stanton have left her to play in the fields of sin here in Troublesome Creek? Kegan would never have done that. He would have put her on a pedestal and worshiped her and kept her safe. That's how he was.

Jayne patted Kegan's hand and smiled at him, as if they had known each other forever. "You're not saying much, Frank," she said.

He realized she had used his first name and made it sound normal. He smiled back at her. "I'm happy for you,

Jayne," he said, using her first name, too. "I'm glad you have your children back."

Their eyes met again and stayed locked until one of the children demanded her attention. She looked over at Garnett. "Thank you for taking care of my kids, Mr. Garnett."

"They're good kids," Garnett replied.

Jayne smiled and replied, "They did run away on me but they meant well, so I'll forgive them."

Kegan turned to Jayne and said, "Now you can go home, can't you?" It sounded like more than a suggestion, it was an urgent warning to get her away from this horrible place to a safer one.

"Yes, that's true. We can go home now," she said looking into Kegan's eyes again, thinking that all she had to go back home to was a drab, cold-water flat on the south side of St. Louis and a job working in a hat factory. She sighed. "Yes, I suppose we can go home now."

"No we can't!" Joy said. "We can't go home just yet!"

"Why not, honey?" Jayne asked.

"Because of Daddy! He came here to get rich for us so you wouldn't have to work, Momma! He died here for us! It ain't right we should give up and run off!"

"But we can't stay here sleeping on the ground and eating out of cans forever," Jayne replied. "Can we?"

"We'll, I ain't goin' back," Ken said stubbornly. "Not yet. Not until I find thet big nugget Daddy was lookin' for."

Jayne smiled sadly. She reached over and caressed Ken's face. "Well, I suppose I could last a week or two more in this wicked place. Would that be enough?"

Ken gave that some thought. "I guess. Would you stay and help us, Mr. Garnett?"

Garnett wasn't expecting the question. It took some thinking, looking for a way to get out of committing himself. He couldn't think of any so finally he said, "Well, I guess I could stay a week more. Maybe our luck will change. You never can tell."

"Only a week?" Joy was disappointed.

"Okay, two weeks, then," Garnett replied. That seemed to satisfy the children.

Later after they had eaten and Jayne and the children were in the buckboard, Kegan took Garnett aside. "Look, Garnett. I'd like it if you sent them back to where they came from. I'll bear the cost, whatever it is."

"Yeah, you're right, Kegan, this is no place for them. I'll have them on a stage in a week or two at most."

"Thanks, Garnett."

"If you don't mind my asking, what's your interest in her?"

Kegan looked away. He was in a fix. He had deep feelings for Jayne Stanton and, unless he misread the signs, she had feelings for him, too. But he had to get past all that. He would never make a family man. Not in his line of work, him being a hired gun most of his life. All he wanted now was for her and the children to be safe.

"We're just good friends, Garnett," Kegan finally said.

"Sure," Garnett replied, but he didn't believe it.

They shook hands and Garnett went out to the buckboard. He got it turned around and they headed for the panning site.

Chapter 9

It was late afternoon when bank robbers Dirk Larsen, Curt Traven, Link Fontaine and Cory Dupree stopped by the side of the road outside Troublesome Creek. They smoked and talked as they passed around a bottle of cheap whiskey.

"What's the plan, boss?" Traven asked Larsen.

"There ain't no plan, Curt," Larsen replied. "We just ride in, find this guy's gold exchange an' rob his ass blind, is all we have ta do."

Link Fontaine and Cory Dupree laughed. Like Curt Traven, they were simple minded men. None of them could read or write, except Larsen. Without him, they were lost sheep. He was the driving force. They'd follow Larsen into the mouth of hell and never give it a thought.

"Look," Larsen went on, "if we all ride into town together, we might attract attention. So, I'll go first. Give me a ten minute head start, then you boys ride in five minutes apart. Go to a saloon and wait there until I come."

"What if they got more than one saloon?" Dupree asked.

"Pick one. I'll find ya. Jest git a table and wait," Larsen said impatiently.

The plan suited them so they nodded in agreement. Larsen could always be counted on to come up with something easy. It didn't take much to confuse them. He knew that and kept things simple. That's why they never got caught.

The outlaw chief left them alongside the road and headed into Troublesome Creek at a slow lope. He walked his horse slowly down the main street of town, looking from side to side, making mental note of where things were located. He also read the signs above the doorways.

The first place on his left, going in, was a mercantile. Larsen noticed a young girl and a boy were stopping there to tie their buckboard to the rail. He laughed. Just some kids going to buy groceries. No threat there. In the center of town, on his left again, Larsen saw Fox's Gold Exchange between a second hand jewelry shop and a boot mender's place. It wasn't much to look at, just wide enough for a door and a window looking out on the main part of town.

Larsen looked for a marshal's office and jail. He saw none and smiled. It was just as he figured, a rag-tag gold field town with no law. It had a bawdy house, a saloon and a Chinese laundry, like all the other prospecting towns he'd seen. He rode through town past Mary Mason's Beanery, Bed and Breakfast to the panning sites. Finding a path that led down to the creek, he stopped at the edge and rolled a cigarette, looking around while his horse drank. He could see the long stretch of places where people were panning and digging for gold. They were scattered along the water's edge for as far as the eye could see.

When he finished smoking, Larsen rode slowly back into town. Seeing the horses of Traven and Fontaine at the Purple Dove Saloon, he tied up to the rail and went in. They were sitting at a table in the back by the wall, waiting. Larsen went over and sat down.

"Where's Dupree?" Larsen asked.

"Damn if I know," Traven said. "You know him. You can't ever tell what he's up to next."

"I bet he went to thet bawdy house up the road," Fontaine said. "He wouldn't pass up a bawdy house if'n his life depended on it. Haw!"

Larsen nodded. Fontaine was right. Dupree had trouble with that sort of thing. It caused a problem more than once. Over in Darby Town, they had to bust him out of jail for molesting a young girl. The same in Johnson's Falls.

"Here he comes now," Traven said, nodding towards the batwing doors. He waved Dupree over to the table.

"Where the hell you been, Dupree?" Larsen asked.

"They got a bawdy house two doors up. I had the urge ta scratch an itch."

"Jesus," Traven said, "you sure must have some bad itch, Dupree."

"Well, it's been a long time," Dupree whined.

"Seems like it was only three days ago ta me," Larsen said. He glared hard at Dupree. "Go git us a bottle and four glasses. An' don't git lost."

As Dupree waddled off towards the bar, Traven said, "Christ, we oughta git rid of the fool. He can't keep his mind on the job."

"No, but he's fast with a gun," Larsen replied. "Darn fast."

Fontaine sniffed. "Yeah, but thet's about all he's good for."

"We'll replace him when the time comes," Larsen replied. "In the meantime, don't git him all riled up. He kin go a little bit crazy."

"Crazy? Hell, he's off his rocker," Traven said. "He's gonna sink us one of these days."

When Dupree came back they drank and smoked.

"So, what did ya find out, boss?" Traven asked Larsen.

"Well, it looks like there ain't no lawmen here."

"How about the gold place?" Fontaine inquired. "Did ya find it?"

"Yeah. He's got one guard jest like I figured," Larsen replied. "The safe is behind the counter where they weigh the gold. It's a pretty simple layout."

"How we gonna do it, boss?" Dupree asked.

"About the same as a bank job," Larsen replied. "Me, Traven and Fontaine go in while you stay with the horses. We git the money and gold and head outta town the way we came in. You bring up the rear."

"How come I gotta bring up the rear, boss?"

"Because yer the fastest with a gun. We depend on you ta watch our backs, Dupree." Larsen knew Dupree was a sucker for a compliment. "Yer the main man, Dupree, the linchpin."

For a moment, Dupree looked confused. "What's a linchpin, boss?"

"It's the most important part of an organization. Without it, the whole works fall apart."

Dupree smiled. He suddenly felt like a big man. "Don't worry about me, boss, I'll be the linchpin. I'll cover yer backs alright."

"Good boy," Larsen said. He had handled Dupree like a baby. "I knew I could count on you, Dupree."

Dupree didn't realize that the last man to leave a job was the first one the posse ran down. Larsen, Traven and Fontaine were well aware of that fact. They smiled knowingly at each other.

"When we gonna do it, boss?" Dupree asked. He was anxious for action, ready to go.

"How about right now?" Larsen said.

"Right now?" Dupree asked.

"Yeah. Right now."

"Alright then, let's do it!" Dupree said, standing up and adjusting his gunbelt.

Traven and Fontaine poured a last shot of whiskey, tossed it down in one pull, and then checked their guns. Larsen grabbed the half full whiskey bottle, and his men followed him outside to the horses. He shoved the bottle in his saddlebag.

From then on everything became routine. It was how they always did it and it worked every time. Nothing fancy for Dirk Larsen and his men. Everything had to be kept simple.

Larsen, Traven and Fontaine walked their mounts across the street slow and casual. Dupree followed a few yards behind. Once on the other side, they stopped at the boot repair shop next to the Gold Exchange and tied up at the rail. Dupree stayed in his saddle in the road, close to the horses, trying to look casual but taking in everything around him. Larsen, Traven and Fontaine stood together pretending to look at the boots for sale in the window of the boot shop.

Larsen whispered, "I'll go look through the window see if there's a customer inside. If it's clear, I'll go in. Traven, you come in fast behind me with yer gun ready. Fontaine, you stay by the door and don't let nobody in." Traven and Fontaine nodded. It was the same old plan. They knew it well.

Just as Larsen approached the Gold Exchange, a prospector came out. Larsen gave him a smile then quickly stepped inside. Traven followed Larsen with his gun drawn. Fontaine stood by the door.

An old man came ambling up the plank sidewalk and stopped at the Gold Exchange, wanting to go in.

"It's closed up, old timer," Fontaine said, waving his gun. The old man knew what was going on. He nodded, turned and scrambled back the way he came.

It was a long time before Larsen and Traven came out. Larsen was in the lead, carrying a sack. In a few seconds, they were mounted and riding fast for the east end of town.

Dupree, who had been looking at a young Chinese girl across the street, was caught off guard. When he realized what was happening, he kicked his mount into a run, trying to catch up with the others. They were a hundred yards ahead of him.

Dodging people as they walked across the street, Dupree made his way up the road. A young girl and a boy, standing beside their buckboard in front of the mercantile, had seen Larsen, Traven and Fontaine ride past. She stared after them, failing to notice Dupree come up behind her. He grabbed her up onto his saddle as if she were light as a feather, and kept on going. She kicked and screamed for help. The boy stood looking helplessly on as the girl disappeared into the distance.

Chapter 10

Mark Fox was boiling over with anger. His bodyguard, Frank Kegan, stood by while two shabby looking gunmen had walked into his Gold Exchange and robbed all his gold and working cash. All told, they'd taken about twenty thousand dollars.

"Why the hell didn't you do something, Kegan?" Fox yelled. "You just stood there with your hands up like a frightened girl! Damn it!"

Kegan shrugged. "They had the drop on us, boss. They'd have killed us both. We're lucky to be alive."

"Well, we'll have to close up shop," Fox said with a sigh. "We're all cleaned out."

He shook his head and stared at Kegan. The man had failed to do his job, which was to protect Fox and his business, even if it meant laying down his life. Instead, he had tossed up his hands and stepped aside as the outlaws cleaned out his safe.

Maybe it was time to cut Kegan loose and find a replacement. As the idea rolled around in his mind, the words suddenly slipped out of Fox's mouth. "Kegan, you're fired!"

"What?" Keagan frowned for a moment, then asked, "What did you say?"

"I said I won't be needing you anymore."

Kegan let the words and their implication settle in for a moment. "You won't be needing me anymore? How come?"

Fox was calmer now. He looked away and said, "I've been thinking about pulling up stakes lately. I'm heading back East. It's too dangerous here. Anyway, I've a feeling this place is about panned out." He was careful not to mention the eighty thousand dollars he had stashed away in his secret bank account in the Cattlemen's Savings and Loan in Scott City.

"So, yer cuttin' me loose?"

"Yes. I've had enough. Too many close calls."

"You owe me a couple of months' back pay. Three, to be exact."

"Well, I'm broke because of you, Kegan, so don't come crying to me for money."

Kegan was about to grab Fox by the collar when Jayne and her son Ken came running up the porch and into the exchange.

"Frank, they took Joy!" Jayne cried.

"Who?" Kegan asked.

"It was four men. They were riding out of town. The last one grabbed her."

"Those were the ones who just robbed me," Fox said.

"I'll go after them." Kegan turned and headed for the porch with Jayne and Ken close behind.

"Kegan!" Fox yelled. "Bring back my money and gold and I'll give you ten percent! And your job back! You hear me?"

Kegan gave no indication he had heard Fox. He looked at Jayne Stanton. "Go get Garnett. Tell him what happened."

Without another word, Kegan ran for the stables to saddle up his horse. In twenty minutes he was galloping up the road past the mercantile and out of town.

Evening was closing in by the time he was an hour out on the road. He looked behind him sometimes to see if Garnett was coming. He'd need help. Four of them were too much for one man. Then were was the girl, Joy. She could get hurt in a wild shootout. No, this was a bad deal from any angle.

Kegan rode on, watching the road up ahead. He began to worry. Maybe they had heard or caught a glimpse of him. They could easily pull off the road and hide until he passed by. But then again, how would they know who he was? For all they knew, he was just a stranger passing by.

As far as a posse was concerned, there was no danger of that and the outlaws knew it. Not unless Fox offered a reward. That would be different, then. Kegan nudged the mustang into a faster gait. Suddenly he heard a girl's voice ahead in the dark. She was screaming but then stopped, as if someone had put a hand over her mouth.

Kegan held his mount at a slower pace, putting more distance between him and the outlaws. He began to think about how best to handle the situation. It was like a game of chess. If the pawn was used right, it could do a lot of damage. One thing was for sure, he had to get them all on the ground because one of them could ride off with the girl while the other three threw down on him.

Well over two hours went by before Kegan heard them pull off the road. He stopped too, sitting in the saddle about fifty yards back, listening to their sounds. Quietly dismounting, he led his horse into a stand of scrub oaks and waited. Minutes later, the glow of a small campfire could be seen in the distance, between the trees. They had settled down for the night.

Kegan walked slowly up the road and stood within earshot of their camp. They were talking among themselves at a normal level until one of them raised his voice.

"Jesus, Dupree, that the hell were you thinking?"

"Aw, shucks, boss. I jest wanna play around wif her, thet's all."

"You can't just go an' pick a girl up like that!"

"She won't be no bother, boss. I'll see to thet."

Another voice said, "Look at her. She's scared ta death, Dupree. You ain't gonna have no fun with thet little girl, you stupid idjit!"

"You shut up, Traven, or I'll bust ya one!"

"Sure you will, you fool." There was a pause. "Tell him, Fontaine. Tell him what a damn fool he is."

"Yer a damn fool, Dupree. Ain't he a fool, boss?"

"All of you, just shut the hell up." There was another pause. "Traven is right, Dupree. You messed up this time. You gotta get rid of her."

"Not until I dance with her, boss. Ya know what I mean?"

"Yeah, I know what you mean, an' that's yer problem, Dupree." Another pause. "Get rid of her!"

"Now?"

"Yeah, now!"

"How? Whatta ya want me ta do?"

"I don't care what you do, just get rid of her, now, you fool!"

Kegan decided to make a move. He walked into the camp site smiling, with his hands in view. "Howdy, fellahs!" They all drew their guns. "Hey! Take it easy. I'm here to help."

"Help? How the hell you gonna help?" Larsen asked.

"I'm gonna take the girl off your hands," Kegan said. chuckling. He looked around. "Where is she?"

"Say, ain't you the one in the Gold Exchange when we robbed it?" Larsen growled.

"Yep. That's me!" Kegan replied.

"Let's drill him," Traven sneered.

"Hell," Fontaine said, "give him the darn girl and let's git the hell outta here. We're wastin' time."

"Yer right about that, friend," Kegan said. "My boss is getting up a posse right now to get his money back. He's put a bounty on your butts."

Joy Stanton's voice came from over by the scrub oaks, in the dark. "I'm over here, Mr. Kegan."

"Are you okay, Joy?"

"I'm somewhat okay."

"Just take it easy, honey I'll have you outta here in a minute."

"Like hell, you will!" Dupree yelled. "Ain't nobody takin' her nowhere, mister! She's gonna dance with me!" He kept is gun leveled at Kegan.

Kegan looked at Larsen. "Is he crazy?"

"Yeah, he's crazy as a loon, mister," Larsen sneered. "But he's also fast on the draw. If you want the girl, you gotta brace him first."

Kegan looked at Dupree, sizing him up. He hadn't expected things to turn like this. If he braced Dupree, then what? It was hard to say. They might let him go, but they might not. But he was in too deep now to back out. He'd have to back up his bluff.

"Okay, Dupree," Kegan said. "I'll brace you for the girl."

"Hell, why should I? I got the drop on you right now, mister!"

Larsen stared at Kegan. The outlaw chief's mind raced. This might be a way to get rid of Dupree and the girl at the same time. But he also knew Dupree was the fastest in the gang and he might drill the intruder, depending on how fast the stranger was. If Dupree won, he and the girl would still be Larsen's problem.

Larsen snickered and started to roll a cigarette. "What's the matter, Dupree? Afraid of this fellah?"

The remark stung Dupree. He looked at his boss and then back at Kegan. He laughed and said, "Hell no. He don't scare me none."

"Then brace him and go dance with the girl."

That pleased Dupree. He smiled. "Okay. I will." His face turned serious and his forehead wrinkled up as he scowled and put his gun away. The others stepped out of the line of fire. "I'm a bracin' you fer thet little girl, mister," Dupree growled. "Draw!"

Dupree went for his gun. It was halfway out of the holster when Kegan's hand came across and fanned off two shots. Dupree's body shuddered and shook. He had a surprised look on his face as he looked down at the two holes in his chest.

"Sweet Jesus!" Traven muttered. He stared at Dupree, then at Kegan.

"I'm daid," Dupree muttered as his legs folded and he fell face down on the ground with a gurgling sigh. His legs twitched twice then stopped.

Larsen, Traven and Fontaine stared down at Dupree's body for a moment, then over at Kegan. Larsen was smiling, happy at the outcome, but the other two weren't.

"He just kilt Dupree, boss," Traven said.

"Yeah. So what? It was fair an' square, wasn't it?"

"Yeah, but I don't like it," Fontaine said. "Dupree was our pard, boss."

"Okay, then you two brace him," Larsen said, pointing his gun in their direction, "but one at a time. We gotta keep it fair. Dupree was askin' fer it an' he got it."

Traven had second thoughts. "Wal, I suppose yer right, when ya put it thet a way, boss."

"Yeah," Fontaine said, "like you said, boss, it was fair an' square."

Larsen was satisfied that Dupree was no longer a problem. He holstered his gun. Traven and Fontaine did the same. It was all over. "Go get the girl, mister."

"Thanks," Kegan said. "I appreciate it." He holstered his gun and started to walk away, then turned back. "Ah, just one more thing."

"What's that?" Larsen asked.

"The money and gold. I'd like to have it, as well."

Larsen was surprised, but he quickly recovered and scowled. "I don't take thet as funny."

"It wasn't meant to be funny," Kegan replied calmly, smiling.

"There's three of us against one of you."

A voice came from the road. "You're wrong about that, friend. It's two to three. That's pretty good odds."

Garnett stepped from the darkness into the light of the campfire. He stood by Kegan's side, his hand down by his Colt.

"I was thinkin' maybe you weren't gonna show up for the party, Garnett," Kegan said, his eyes on the three outlaws, his hand poised by his gun.

"You take the big one, I'll take the other two," Garnett said.

"Naw, let me have those two," Kegan said.

"You sure?" Garnett asked.

"Yep, I'm sure."

Larsen drew. He was fast and got off a shot that put a hole in Garnett's shirt sleeve, near his shoulder. Garnett's return shot hit him between the eyes snapping his head back. His body went flying into the darkness, out in the brush. Garnett dipped low and spun to the right.

He heard Kegan's gun bark once and saw his bullet take Traven high in the chest, knocking him twisting and turning until his legs got jammed up and he fell backwards.

Fontaine took that split second to blindside Kegan with a sneak shot, hitting him above the elbow, on his left arm. That prevented Kegan from fanning off a shot but he managed to thumb one into Fontaine's leg just as Garnett put a bullet in Fontaine's heart.

It took the echoes of gunfire a few moments to fade away before the sounds of the night returned.

"You hurt bad?" Garnett asked.

"No. Go get Joy. She's over by the horses, tied to a tree."

Garnett quickly found her. He untied her and brought her into the light, near the fire. She shivered when she saw the dead bodies. She pointed at Dupree. "He was the one who took me."

"Are you alright?" Kegan asked.

Joy nodded. "Yes, I'm alright, Mr. Kegan, but you're hurt."

Garnett walked over to Kegan and tore his shirt sleeve open to get a look at the wound. It was slight. "You came up lucky, Kegan. The heat of the bullet cauterized it."

"I'm fine," Kegan replied.

He walked over into the shadows where the horses were tied to some scrub oaks, got Larsen's saddlebag and brought it back. He whistled and a moment later his mustang came trotting up the road. Kegan tied the outlaw chief's saddlebag over his own.

"Your boss' money, huh?" Garnett asked.

"Yeah," Kegan replied. He looked around at the bodies. "We'd better get out of here. Anybody coming along the road will stop to ask questions."

"Yeah," Garnett said "It might be hard to explain all this."

They got the outlaw horses lined up in a convoy. Joy climbed up on Larsen's horse and they headed back to Troublesome Creek. It stayed dark for a few hours and then the first signs of dawn cracked the horizon. After a while they heard the sounds, smells and smoke of Troublesome Creek.

Chapter 11

Mark Fox had a low opinion of Chinese people. He was ignorant of their historical accomplishments and considered them inferior people. Even so, he didn't mind having an affair with the laundryman's beautiful wife, Mae Wan. As far as feelings went, he had no deep affection for this beautiful young girl. He could love no one but himself and his money. She was simply a fancy, a desire, a way to satisfy his baser impulses. She meant nothing to him.

On her part, she thought his intentions were sincere. He had no wife and she seemed to be the only woman he was involved with. She was skillful and knew how to satisfy his carnal needs and he regularly enjoyed her special abilities in that field. Her hope was that Fox might someday take her away from her squalid existence in Troublesome Creek, a place she hated.

Whenever Fox wanted Mae Wan to come to him, he would take an article of clothing to the laundry, and hand it over the counter to her and nod. The nodding part was the signal that he wanted to see her. Their eyes would meet and she would know he wanted her to come to the back room of the Gold Exchange after dark. She thought of it as their private little love nest.

Her old husband, Huang Ling, knew about the affair but couldn't get up the courage to do anything about it. In his mind, he was but a lowly laundryman and Fox was an important man in town. He was the richest and most powerful man in Troublesome Creek and could squash the Chinaman like a bug.

But Huang Ling's ancient mother did not fear Fox. To her, he was a detestable white ghost.

"She sneaks out at night, my son, when you start to snore," the old lady whispered in her son's ear. "She consorts with the vile white ghost!" Huang Ling would only shrug the words off and continue with his work. It was best to keep busy and not think about it.

One day, his mother took him aside and fired off an ultimatum. "This disgrace cannot be tolerated anymore. It is an insult to our ancestors. Their spirits are crying out from the grave for you to do something."

"But what can I do, Mother?"

"Have you no backbone? Must I do it for you?"

Huang Ling began to sob. The situation had been torturing him for over a year, now. He saw no end to it. He dreaded to think that Mae Wan might leave him for this other man. It would kill him if she did. He loved her more than anything in the world, but he also feared being disgraced in front of his mother and ancestors.

"You must follow her the next time," his mother said. "You must confront this white ghost!"

"How? In what way?" Huang Ling asked, sobbing pitifully.

Huang Ling's mother reached into an ornate chest of drawers and took out a knife with a long, thin blade. She handed it to her son. Huang Ling nodded. He knew he could offer no further excuses. Now was the time to act. He could stall no more. Later that night he followed his young wife for the first time. He vowed it would be the last time because he was determined to resolve the situation and put it to rest. His family's honor demanded he do so.

Outside, in the dark, she was easy to follow as she ran down one alley and up another in her sheer white chemise. Finally, Mae Wan came to her destination, the back room of the Gold Exchange, a short way from the laundry. She opened the door, went in, and locked it behind her. The old man looked through a small window near the door.

By the pale glow of an oil lamp he watched them. Tears ran down his face and, to keep from screaming in rage, he bit his lip until it bled. Finally, he turned away, sat on the ground and sobbed quietly. He could bear to watch no more. The betrayal had cut too deep.

Minutes passed and he heard them talking. Their voices were not soft and sweet like lovers, but loud and angry. Huang Ling got up and looked through the window again. He could easily hear every word they spoke. Fox was dressed now and he stood smoking a cigar while he waited for Mae Wan to finish putting on her chemise.

"You should go before your husband finds out what an unfaithful wife you are," Fox said sarcastically.

"I am with child," Mae Wan said. "I am never going back to him again. You must take me."

"No, you can't stay with me!" Fox insisted.

100

"Yes, I will stay with you. I am yours now."

"It doesn't work that way. You have to go back to him."

"No, I won't. I can't stand for the old man to touch me."

"I won't be tied down. Anyway, I'm leaving this place."

"Take me with you or I shall tell everyone in town I am with your child."

"You'll what?"

"You heard me!"

"Are you threatening me?"

"If I must, yes!"

Fox tossed his cigar aside and glared at Mae Wan. His face was flushed with anger.

"We're finished," he said, walking to the door and pulling back the latch. "Get out! It's over!"

Mae Wan lunged at Fox, raking her fingernails down the side of his face. He gasped in pain and shoved her hard against the wall. With a grunt, she rushed back at him again trying to get at his eyes. They closed together in combat. She lashed out at him with her long, sharp fingernails, cutting his face again. They struggled, entwined like two snakes. He finally got his hands around her throat and squeezed with all his strength.

It took a while but she stopped resisting. The rage in her eyes vanished as they went blank. Even then, Fox kept squeezing until she was as limp as a rag.

Outside, Huang Ling watched the white ghost kill the wife he loved but who had betrayed him. A mixture of hate, fear, and confusion came over him. Holding the knife up, he stared at its long, pointed blade. Footsteps sounded and he realized the white ghost was coming out. The Chinaman shrunk back into the shadows and watched Fox walk down the alley with the body of Mae Wan hanging over his shoulder. She looked like a tiny doll, her white chemise fluttering in the wind and her arms dangling down.

Huang Ling followed them quietly through the alley, behind some buildings and through a stand of willow trees. The sound of water nearby told him they were not far from the creek. He knew then what the white ghost was going to do.

Fox walked into the creek up to his ankles and lowered the body of Mae Wan into the water. The current grabbed it from his hands and took it, slowly wending downstream. In the ghostly moonlight, her white, sheer chemise fluttered on the updraft, as if waving goodbye. The whitecaps of the water sparkled like diamonds all around the girl's body.

"Goodbye, baby," Fox chuckled. "Have a nice trip."

As Fox started to turn around, he felt a pain in his back. It was so sudden it took his breath away. He coughed as something sharp kept going in and out, working its way down to his ribs. He tasted blood in his mouth and then the next thing he knew he was face down in the cold waters of Troublesome Creek. After that, there was nothing to see, hear or feel.

A few yards downstream, the body of Mae Wan snagged on a low hanging tree branch. She waited with open arms as Fox's body collided with hers and they both headed for Colorado. Somewhere in the hills beyond Troublesome Creek, a band of coyotes howled a mournful funeral dirge to announce the death of two lovers and the foul deed that was done.

Chapter 12

It was daylight when Garnett, Kegan and Joy Stanton rode slowly back into Troublesome Creek with the four outlaw horses and the stolen money and the gold. Roosters crowed and dogs barked to announce their arrival. The little caravan stopped at the stable on the east edge of town and woke up the stableman.

"Looks like ya got them varmints, Frank," Tom Parker, the blacksmith, said with a yawn.

"We did, Tom," Kegan said. "This is their horses and gear. Sell it off and take forty percent."

"Forty percent? Heck, yes," the stableman said. "Be glad ta do thet, Frank."

"I figured you would, Tom."

They left the outlaw horses with the blacksmith. Joy mounted up behind Garnett, and they continued riding straight through town to the Stanton panning site. When they got there, Joy jumped down and ran into her mother's waiting arms.

"Thank you," Jayne said to Garnett and Kegan. "I'll never forget what you two did." She suddenly noticed Kegan's wound. "Frank, you're hurt! Get down and I'll take a look at it."

"It's not much," Kegan said. He dismounted and sat on the old log near the big tent as Jayne went inside.

Kegan looked around at the panning site. For a moment, he felt a wave of guilt as he visualized John Stanton struggling with the wheelbarrow full of dirt as he dug for gold all alone. Now he was gone and only Kegan and Fox knew why. The gunman shook the vison from his mind as Jayne came out of the tent with a small medicine box.

"What's wrong, Frank?" she asked.

"Nothing, Jayne. I guess I'm a little tired."

Jayne looked at him for a moment, nodded, then went to work cleaning and dressing the wound. "It should be okay," she said when she was finished.

Garnett stood a few feet away rolling a cigarette. He noticed the intimacy between the two and smiled, thinking they looked good together. Kegan got up. Walking over to his horse, he mounted then leaned back and patted the top saddlebag. "Guess I'll get this back to Fox."

"Yeah, he's probably worried to death," Garnett said.

"Yeah," Kegan replied with a look of sarcasm on his face. He saluted Jayne, turned his horse and rode back into town.

"I'm hungry," Ken Stanton said. "Can we go eat at the beanery?"

Before Jayne could answer, Garnett replied cheerfully, "Sure we can! Let's go, it's on the house." Garnett smiled at Jayne. He knew her finances were low.

"Thank you, Mr. Garnett," she said.

Hitching the horse to the buckboard, they loaded up and headed towards the beanery. It was just opening and a lot of prospectors were jammed at the door. Garnett was lucky enough to find a table by the window where it was warm. They ordered breakfast.

"You have been very kind to me," Jayne said to Garnett. "I don't know how I can ever repay you, Mr. Garnett."

"You already have, ma'am."

"I have? How?"

"By coming here and getting your children. Some people wouldn't bother. It tells me a lot about you, ma'am."

Jayne smiled. "Thank you for the compliment, Mr. Garnett."

As they ate breakfast, Garnett heard loud whispering going on among the prospectors. It was like the buzzing of bees, rising and falling in waves. Words like "new", "big" and "strike" floated on the air. He also noticed that buckboards loaded with tents and equipment were going slowly past the window, traveling east out of town.

"It looks like something's going on," Garnett said to Jayne.

Just then, Kegan came in, looking around. Seeing Jayne and the others, he walked up to the table. He still had the saddlebags. As he pulled a chair up to the table, he hung them over the back and sat down.

Garnett asked, "Couldn't find your boss, huh?"

"No," Kegan said. He stared hard at Garnett and Garnett wondered why.

Jayne glanced out the window at the passing column of people. "I wonder what that's all about?"

"I don't know," Garnett replied. "Looks like they're leaving."

Mary Mason came over to take Kegan's order.

"What's goin' on, Mary?" Kegan asked.

"There's been a big strike up on the Colorado border, near a place called Pike's Peak."

"What about here?" Garnett asked.

"It's about played out," Mary said. "It ain't what it once was. Too many people, too little gold and too much killin'. It happens all the time."

"Will they all leave?" Jayne asked.

"Some might hang around for a while. But not for long. They'll get the itch an' head out fer this new place."

They ate breakfast while watching the exodus. A steady column of people rolled slowly past the beanery window. Some were in buckboards piled high with their belongings, and others rode by with pack horses trailing behind. Many walked slowly along with loads on their backs, leading stubborn mules. Sometimes there was a break in the line, but not for long as others hurried to fill the gap.

Kegan laughed. "What's so funny, Frank?" Jayne asked.

"I was just thinking. Fox and me, we've been through this a few times before."

An angry looking man came in with an armful of dirty clothes. When he spotted Mary, he walked over to her and said, "Darn it! Jest when I done run outta fresh red flannels."

Mary said, "What's the matter, Bill? You look like ya swallowed a live frog."

"It's them Chinese, they done pulled up stakes!"

"You mean they're gone?" Mary replied with skepticism.

"Yep! Flew the coop, lock, stock and barrel!"

"You sure?"

"Yep. Funny thing is, all the laundry is done! Laid out on the counter with tags on it."

"That don't mean they're gone, Bill. Maybe they're takin' a day off, is all."

"Well, they took everything with them, then. All the tubs and machinery is gone. So are the wagons. Ain't nobody there."

Mary chuckled. "I guess they heard about that gold strike over in Colorado, then."

Jayne turned to Kegan. "I suppose that means Mr. Fox will be leaving, too, then."

"Yes, I suppose so," Kegan muttered. Garnett saw that strange look on his face again.

"I guess that means you'll be leaving as well, doesn't it?" Jayne asked. Kegan didn't answer. He looked away. After that, they ate in silence.

An hour later they all went back to the panning site. Kegan motioned for Garnett to join him by the side of the creek. They talked as they rolled cigarettes and smoked.

"I see you still got the saddlebags with the money," Garnett said.

"Yeah."

"What's that all about?"

"It's about Fox. He's dead."

Garnett frowned. "Dead? Are you sure?"

"Yeah. I checked his room behind the Gold Exchange. Looked like there'd been a scuffle. Table and chairs overturned. Blood on the floor. There were footprints outside. I followed them into the woods."

"Boots?"

"No, sandals, like the Chinese wear."

"Where'd the footprints go to?"

"Down to the creek. There was a lot of blood on some rocks there, too. Close to the edge."

"So, what do you think happened?"

"Fox has been messin' with the old Chinaman's pretty young wife for a year, now. I figure the Chinaman finally got fed up an' decided to put an end to it."

"I see," Garnett replied thoughtfully. "So, where's that leave you, Frank?"

Kegan looked over at Jayne and the kids where they were sitting on the old log. "Right where I wanna be. With her and the kids."

"What about the money?"

"I figure you and me earned it. We'll split it. Is that okay with you?"

"Yeah, sure. It's ours, now, I suppose," Garnett said. "How much cash is in there?" He nodded at the saddlebags.

"About ten thousand in cash and ten thousand in gold."

Garnett gave the matter some thought, then said. "Just give me two thousand."

"Only two grand? Are you sure?"

"Yeah. You and her are gonna need the rest of it."

"Thanks, Garnett. I appreciate it."

Twenty yards away, out on the road, the stream of people kept winding slowly and steadily along. Each one seemed eager to go on to the next adventure. Some were singing songs, while others were joking and laughing.

Jayne got up from the log and walked over to Kegan and Garnett. "How long do you think this will go on?" Jayne asked.

"At least three more days," Kegan replied.

"We'll wait and leave then," Jayne said, looking into his eyes.

"I suppose you're going back to St. Louis?" the gunman asked.

Jayne hesitated, then relied, "I suppose so. There's no place else to go. I can't stay here. What about you, Frank?"

Kegan shrugged. "That depends."

"On what?"

"I've always wanted to buy a small ranch in Wyoming and raise cattle."

"That sounds wonderful," Jayne replied. "But you're not a cowboy."

"I was, once, for a while. Anyway, I'd hire cowhands to run it."

Garnett walked away and sat on the log, listening to them talk, smiling to himself. Ken went to toss rocks into the creek and Joy went into the tent, leaving him sitting alone.

"It sounds wonderful, Wyoming, fresh air and all. The children would like going to a place like that," he heard Jayne say. It was an opening invitation to Kegan, if he was looking for one.

Kegan jumped on it. "If that's the case, why don't you come along with me?" he said. "We could find a preacher on the way, if you want."

Jayne looked into the gunman's eyes and smiled. "Do you mean that, Frank? Is that what you want?"

"Yes, I mean it. It's what I want." He took her hand and held it.

They stood close together with Troublesome Creek behind them, staring at each other, not knowing what to do next. Finally, Jayne said, "Let me talk it over with Ken and Joy."

"Alright."

They went back to Mary Mason's Beanery twice that day, for lunch and supper. Kegan insisted on paying. At nightfall, Kegan went up to his room above the beanery and the rest of them stayed at the panning site. Ken slept with Garnett in his tent, while Joy and her mother slept in the big one.

Two days later the stableman sold all the outlaw horses, saddles, and gear. He gave six hundred to Kegan and kept four hundred for himself. Kegan split that with Garnett and then gave him two thousand from the Gold Exchange money, too. With the money he already had stashed away, Garnett now had more than eight thousand dollars. Enough to start a small business of his own someday.

They were among the last to pack up their belongings and leave Troublesome Creek. Kegan tied the horse Garnett had given to Ken behind the buckboard, along with his own. He and Jayne sat on the bench and Joy and Ken sat in back amongst the tents, blankets, and gear. They were ready to go.

"You folks headin' for Wyoming, are you?" Garnett asked, as if he didn't know.

"Yup," Kegan said. "The land is open for homesteading and the cattle are running wild like locusts."

"Well, good luck," Garnett said.

"And to you, too, Mr. Garnett," Jayne said. "I'll name one for you."

"I'd be honored, ma'am."

They left Garnett standing in the empty panning site, listening to the roar of Troublesome Creek as its raging waters headed west towards Colorado. He looked around, but there was nothing to see except deserted gold sites. Sitting on the log, he rolled a cigarette and stared out at the roiling, angry water of Troublesome Creek. He wondered how many human souls it had claimed. No, it had not committed any crimes, it was innocent. It was man who did it, he was the culprit who used the raging creek to cover his own atrocities. How many had been committed? Only God had seen and counted.

Later, Garnett went up to Mary Mason's place and sat watching the exodus. He sat there for an hour, then walked around town, watching businesses closing their doors. Later, he ended up back at the beanery, eating and talking to some of the prospectors. He listened as they told him about other gold strikes they had been to. As darkness fell, Garnett took a room up over the beanery for the night.

In the morning, Garnett went back down to eat breakfast. "This is the last meal," Mary said. "After this, I'm closing down and headin' out."

He said goodbye and rode back to the Stanton site to take one last look. After that, he joined the last few stragglers as they rode up the main street of town. He could still hear the creek gurgling behind him. When he came up to Mary

Mason's Beanery, he stopped. A sign nailed to the door said it was closed for business, so he rode on.

All the shops were closed now. Fox's Gold Exchange already had a broken window and the door was wide open. It swung back and forth as if controlled by an invisible hand, creaking on its hinges. The Purple Dove Saloon and Newman's Pleasure House were now empty shells. There was a sadness about them. Many of their windows were also broken, and their batwing doors had been torn off and tossed into the street. Grant's mercantile was boarded up. Its loading dock was bare.

It began to rain hard. It came suddenly. Garnett glanced up and saw that a bank of dark, gray clouds were hanging overhead, just sitting there as if for his personal aggravation. He chuckled and headed his horse for the Purple Dove Saloon. Once there, he tied up at the rail, climbed the porch steps and rushed inside.

Standing in the doorway, Garnett rolled a cigarette, watching the rain, thinking of what he should do and where he should go next. His reveries were suddenly broken by the sound of feet rushing up behind him. As he turned to look, something hit him in the left shoulder and sent him spinning out onto the porch. It was a big man with a pickaxe handle.

As Garnett landed on his back, his hand found his gun and he drew. The man was coming at him fast. Garnett thumbed off a shot and hit the man in the heart. Rolling to one side, he let the body go by. It tumbled off the porch and into the road.

Another man appeared in the doorway. He carried a crowbar and swung it at Garnett. It narrowly missed his head as, still on his back, he fanned off another shot, hitting this one in the left side. Instead of stopping him, it only made the man angrier. He bellowed like a bull and jumped at Garnett in an attempt to kick him in the face. Garnett shot him again, this time in the chest. The man grunted and fell to his knees on the porch. He tried to get up so Garnett shot him again, this time in the head. The third shot did the trick. The man fell flat and didn't move anymore.

"Jesus!" Garnett muttered. He sat up and looked around. No one else was coming, so he got on his feet, reloaded his gun and picked up his hat. He glanced down at the two bodies, shook his head and sighed.

Climbing into the saddle, Garnett rode slowly up the street. He glanced back at the saloon one last time and shrugged. His mind tried to make sense of it, but couldn't. It had been an unexplainable close call with death. Life was like that.

It stopped raining and the air turned colder. Garnett felt an eerie quietness, as if the town were grieving. A feeling of melancholy flowed from the place. It was as if Troublesome Creek was mourning the loss of humanity and feared the fate it knew was coming.

Without the prospectors, Troublesome Creek would slowly shrivel up and die. The heat, the cold, the wind and the rain would attack it relentlessly, day after day. The wood that formed its buildings would dry and split and twist as it was assaulted by natural elements. Roofs would soon begin to buckle and split open, letting in the rain and snow. Tumbleweed and bunchgrass would would fight for dominance. They would clog the streets and alleyways and grow inside places that only humans once claimed.

Without humans to repair it, the town would decay and atrophy and finally die. It would become a ghost town, all but forgotten. At night, coyotes would roam freely in its emptiness. Their loud nocturnal howling would rise up in the night until the moon above trembled in fear.

Troublesome Creek would eventually become lost and forgotten. At best, it would become a footnote in some historian's chronicle, a chronicle that few, if any, would ever read. It would lay gathering dust in some small town library on the west Kansas plains.

That was the fate awaiting Troublesome Creek.

Once on the high ground, Garnett stopped to stare down at the dead, empty shell of Troublesome Creek. He watched as a solitary figure led a pack mule slowly along the road. It was a bent over old man, the last poor soul to leave Troublesome Creek. As the last prospector reached the edge of town, Garnett thought he heard Troublesome Creek let out a mournful sigh, but he realized it was only the wind.

A bank of clouds came overhead and a cold breeze brushed against Garnett's back. He looked up and nodded. Troublesome Creek was in for more rain. The creation of a ghost town was already starting. Garnett turned the big appaloosa and rode east, putting his back to the past.

About fifteen miles east, on the road to Ellis, he stopped at a stagecoach way station to buy a nosebag of grain for his horse and get out of the rain. Because of the nasty weather, the place was packed. Garnett found a place at the bar and ordered a flip-top. It was aptly named Muddy River, but was drinkable.

As he stood there eating shelled boiled eggs in brine, pickled cucumbers and sipping his beer, Garnett listened to the talk going on around him. The conversation of two cowboys on his right arrested his attention.

The tall, skinny one was telling the short, stocky one, "I hear tell she's offerin' a thousand bucks reward."

"Yer crazy, Zack! There ain't nobody offerin' no thousand bucks reward," the short one replied.

"Well, thet's the rumor goin' around, Vern," the tall one said.

"Where's this happenin'?"

"Over in Easton's Corners."

"Hell, thet's nothin' but a one-horse town. It ain't but a pimple on a hog's butt. There ain't nobody lives there that's got a thousand dollars ta give away. Thet's loco talk."

The tall one shrugged and took another drink of red eye. "Yeah, yer probably right."

121

That ended that part of the conversation. From then on, they talked about cows, horses and, eventually, painted ladies. Garnett listened quietly as he ate and drank. Zack and Vern finally left.

Garnett cornered the barman and asked, "Where's Easton's Corners?"

"Easton's Corners? It about a three day due north on the Oakley road." He looked at Garnett's worn wool suit, the one they gave him when he got out of prison. "You a cowboy?" the barman asked, already knowing the answer.

"No."

"Then you wouldn't like it there, unless yer a gambler. Are you a gambler?"

Garnett smiled and replied, "Me? No, I'm just a drifter."

"I take it by yer attire you jest got outta prison. Am I right?"

"You're right, friend," Garnett said. He tossed an eagle on the bar and walked outside.

It stopped raining and there was blue starting to show above. Garnett walked over to the appaloosa and rubbed its ears. It snickered and nudged him. Garnett chuckled, untied the reins from the rail and eased up into the saddle.

"Let's head for Easton's Corners, old pal," he said. "See what all the fuss is about."

Garnett rode east under a clearing sky wondering who "she" was. He was eager to find out. A few miles on and he began to think of the eight thousand dollars he had hidden in the secret pockets of his saddlebags. It was the most money he ever had and he thought about what to do with it. Unlike Kegan, he had no desire to become a cattle rancher. No, he preferred a business that kept him out of the elements. A dry, warm place to spend the rest of his life, like a mercantile or a saloon. And it would be nice to find a woman to share it with.

Kegan had found his woman in Jayne Stanton. Garnett wondered where, when and if he would find his. It would be nice to stop drifting on the wind.

The End

SHOOTOUT AT THE SNAKE PIT

Excerpt

The marshal and Mrs. Garth followed the woman into the kitchen. Garnett stood poised, staring at the door latch, waiting for it to move. In a few seconds, it gave a twitch and the door flew open. Two big, burly men burst into the room. One had a sawed-off shotgun and the other had an old pistol.

Garnett flipped the table up and dropped down behind it just as the shotgun went off. He felt the impact of the lead buckshot as it slammed against the wood. Splinters flew everywhere. The lamp that had been on the table shattered on the sod floor. It went out as the oil soaked into the dirt, casting the room in darkness.

The man with the gun fired several shots at the table. The bullets passed through, narrowly missing Garnett's shoulder. After that he heard the hammer falling on empty chambers.

Garnett quickly stood up. The light from the kitchen showed the two attackers were still standing in the doorway, twenty feet away. He fanned off two quick shots into each man's chest. The force of the bullets slammed them back out into the street.

More gunfire could be heard down the road. Garnett ran outside, jumped over the two bodies, and headed for the saloon. When he got there it was pitch black inside except for the flash of guns. He waited outside as the fight went on for a few seconds longer, then stopped. He waited a minute before yelling, "Anybody in there?"

Rick Pruitt yelled back, "Yeah! Come on in!"

Garnett walked in with his gun drawn. He saw a man behind the bar lighting a lamp and looking pale and shaken. The place was a mess. Tables were overturned and chairs were scattered everywhere. Bodies lay on the floor and some were draped over tables and chairs. Garnett counted eight of them.

Western books by R. Annan

Fight for the Lazy M
The Red Bandana
The Salvation of Trace Logan
The Cowboy from Sierra Blanca

Jack Cordell Westerns

The Gunfighter in Winter
Long Ride to Hell's Kitchen
Owl Hawks
Gunfight at Barfield Springs
Shootout at Sanctuary City
Last Days of a Gunfighter

Clay Jared Westerns

Copperhead Moon
Cowboys of the Box R
Prisoners of Brimstone Pass
Range War in C Minor
Devil Wind
Showdown at Wamego Falls
Lightning Riders
Winter Kill
Gunfight at Wild River
Shootout at Rattlesnake Flats

Jesse Garnett Westerns

Gunfight at Black Bear Lair
Gunfight at Latigo Junction
Outcasts of Troublesome Creek

About the Author

As a young boy growing up in the city, R. Annan never passed up a chance to see a western movie. His heroes were Buck Jones, Johnny Mack Brown, Wild Bill Elliot and John Wayne, to name a few. As an adult he often wondered where his love of westerns came from. Perhaps it has something to do with his grandfather, John L. Annan, who was a cowboy from Helena, Montana, in days of old.

R. Annan is a seasoned and traveled author with many interests. As a career serviceman he served in Korea and Vietnam. He also completed a one-year course at the Defense Language Institute in Monterey, California, and graduated from the University of South Florida with a B.A. in Art and Art History. After taking a two-year course in screenwriting at the Hollywood Scriptwriting Institute, he established The Old Time Radio Club Time Machine as both a scriptwriter and an actor.

A Note from the Author

Thank you for reading my book. If you enjoyed it, would you please consider rating and reviewing it? I'd enjoy your feedback. Thank you!